"Miranda," James said, looking distinctly amused. "What's the matter? Afraid I'll drag you into the lake with me?"

Stepping back, Miranda winced, the back of her knees colliding with the stone bench. "Ha! Afraid you'll drip all over my skirts, more like. Why are you here?"

He flashed a rakish grin. "I thought that obvious. Care for a dip? The water's lovely and you do look rather flushed."

"Certainly not!" she said, her cheeks blazing all the more. "Don't you have your own lake to dabble in—in *Kent*?"

"Why would I travel that far when all I could wish for is right here? And I must say, from this standpoint, one couldn't want for a better view."

Miranda couldn't speak—couldn't think—with him looking at her thusly. As if she were a tall glass of iced lemonade on a midsummer's day. Although icy was the last word she'd use to describe herself at that moment.

He reached out, and her eyes fluttered shut to feel his cool fingertips against her fevered cheek.

Without thought, she leaned into his caress.

Oh no, no, no. This wouldn't do at all!

By Melissa Finch

IN WANT OF AN EARL

IN WANT OF AN EARL

IN WANT OF AN EARL

MELISSA FINCH

Edited by Rania Battany

Cover design by Melissa Reid

Print Edition ISBN: 978-0-6459548-0-7
Digital Edition ISBN: 978-0-6459548-1-4

First Edition: December 2025

For Paul, always.

1

The Cumberland's Ballroom, Mayfair, Spring 1813

And just like that, there he was, waltzing into Lady Cumberland's ballroom without so much as a by your leave. Miss Miranda Drayton blinked, hoping her eyes were deceiving her. But there was no mistaking those windswept curls or that easy grin. Features she'd once foolishly held dear.

Anticipation swept the ballroom as Lady Cumberland hastened forward in welcome. His unexpected appearance was sure to be the talk for many a day to come. Miranda felt ill just at the thought.

Why the devil did he have to return now? When everything was about to fall into place?

Suppressing a shudder, Miranda turned and stiffened to find her younger sister's probing gaze.

"Are you well, Mira?" Lucinda demanded in her typical no-nonsense fashion. "As you look decidedly...odd."

Hearing this, their mother, Lady Nora, glanced over and cooed in concern. "Lucinda is right, my dear, you do look dreadfully pale." She reached down to her ornately tasseled reticule and plucked out a small vial. "Here, take my smelling salts."

Miranda waved the abomination aside. "No need for that, Mother. I am perfectly well. The heat caught up with me for a moment, that is all."

Thankfully, her mother accepted the excuse without question.

She safely stowed the vial and retrieved her fan with a frown. "Oppressive, isn't it? How's one to breathe, let alone enjoy oneself in such a crush is beyond me."

"And yet, the mark of any good hostess seems dependent on the sheer volume of guests she can squeeze into one room," Miranda said dryly, opening her own fan and darting her gaze to the crowd.

She needn't have worried, though. In the short span of their conversation, a wall of feathers had virtually surfaced right before them, obscuring the entranceway from view.

The Cumberland's rout was considered so *de rigueur* that everyone who was anyone was in attendance. Invitation optional, apparently.

A fine thing too, Miranda decided. If she were careful, she might lose herself to the crowd entirely. Ladies were known to misplace their husbands at these events and not recover them until well into the following evening. Inadvertently, at that.

She would just pretend she hadn't seen him. Out of sight, and all.

Her sister's reaction to the mounting speculation, however, was proving harder to ignore.

Lucinda went straight to her toes, craning her neck so as to quickly pinpoint the source of all the fanfare.

"It's James," she gushed. "*Oh, my!*"

'Oh my', indeed. And Lucinda wasn't alone in the sentiment. Heartfelt sighs and appreciative titters were being shared abound. Amongst those of the gentler persuasion most particularly.

Save their mother, perhaps, who only asked absently, "James who, dear?"

"The Earl James Stanton, of course!" Lucinda proclaimed as if there were no other 'James' in the whole of Christendom.

Their mother lowered her fan and smiled. "So, it is. Why, we haven't seen him in an age."

Three years, four months, and fifteen days to be precise. Which was no small feat considering James' godmother, the Dowager Duchess of Winchester, just so happened to be Miranda's aunt. Indeed, they'd all shared many a summer at her aunt's country estate, Rose Manor, James' visits often coinciding with Miranda's own. Much to her delight at the time.

But that was before the Never-To-Be-Mentioned-Again-Incident. Before she went and ruined everything.

Miranda shook her head to dispel the reminder.

Surely none of this was real, and she would awaken at any moment. And by the sounds of it, her mother was similarly bemused.

"I wonder at his presence this evening," she said.

Despite having endured many such events since her come-out, Lady Nora had never understood the appeal of a ball when one could be enjoying a quiet evening at home in its place. Although James had hardly spent these past years resuscitating at his townhouse if the gossips were at all to be believed.

"Why, he must be in want of a wife!" Lucinda directed at their mother and everyone else who happened to be in the vicinity. She then jostled Miranda aside in her quest for a better view. "He's more impressive than my memory rightly serves and is sure to have his pick of this season's incomparables," she continued blithely before turning back to face them. "Wouldn't you agree, Mira? You've been curiously circumspect on the subject thus far, you being James' particular favorite and all."

Fighting back a flush, Miranda lifted her shoulder in lieu of a reply.

If only her sister knew.

Looking back to the man in question, she discovered they were now in clear sight thanks to her sister's maneuverings.

In that next moment James found her, and her cheeks heated at the responding quirk to his lips.

The arrogance!

It seemed some things didn't change.

But then, a certain measure of pride could only be expected. Coming into the title at a relatively young age, he'd always borne it well. His mere appearance in his finely tailored tailcoat, snug-fitting breaches, and artfully tussled hair was plenty enough to have the ladies all aflutter. Unfortunately, he knew only too well the effect he wielded, seemingly without the slightest effort.

Miranda snapped her fan shut.

For all his rumored carousing one would've expected his appearance to have suffered as a result. But vexingly, it wasn't the case. James looked as hearty and hale as he had back at Rose Manor; when he'd stolen her off onto adventures unknown.

Though his shoulders seemed a mite broader than she remembered, and those impossibly tight trousers only emphasized his shapely...

Miranda raised her eyes only to be ensnared by his clearly amused ones. As if he'd somehow discerned the direction of her thoughts.

Narrowing her gaze, she mentally consigned him to the Devil. To anywhere really, provided it was nowhere near wherever she was.

Refusing to back down, she matched him glare for glare. Until the familiar jingle of medallions had her severing eye contact.

She could hardly ignore the colonel's approach; the man had sired her after all.

Turning, Miranda straightened to see that her father had Lord Sommerville and his son, Viscount Hawthorne, right alongside him. With that, she pushed all thoughts of James Stanton aside.

The past didn't matter. How could it when her future was marching straight toward her? Lord Hawthorne—her soon-to-be betrothed—in all his immaculate glory.

Provided everything went according to plan, of course.

"My dears," the colonel said in such a tone, one couldn't help but stand to attention. "Look who I managed to salvage from the crush."

"Good evening, my lords," Lady Nora said, dipping into a deep curtsy.

Miranda and Lucinda were quick to mirror the action, offering their own greetings in turn.

Lord Sommerville dipped his head, losing his chin to his cravat in the process. "Ladies, why how lovely you look. Yes indeed, t'is a lovely evening all round."

"That it is," Miranda responded, seeing her mother had become distracted by another bout of fan waving. "And you, Lord Hawthorne?" she said, turning to the viscount. "How are you enjoying the ball thus far? I have found the quartet to be especially talented."

"Lady Cumberland has exacting taste, and this season has proven no exception. One need only look to the caliber of her guestlist," he returned, the deep timbre to his voice drawing a soft sigh from Lucinda.

An entirely understandable reaction. Uncommonly handsome, Lord Hawthorne sported a full mane of dark hair and an aquiline nose that only drew attention to the strong line of his jaw.

But whilst Miranda could appreciate a fine form as much as the other, she found his nature all the more compelling. The viscount was completely without artifice. A true valiant as her father liked to say. Thus, she wasn't the least surprised when he declined a glass of claret from a passing footman and kept his steady gaze trained her way.

Before he could speak, though, Lucinda chimed in. "Speaking of guests, Lord Hawthorne, did you happen to—"

Fortunately, the quartet picked up their bows, gifting Miranda the perfect opening to step forward. "Our dance, I believe," she directed at the viscount.

She couldn't say for certain what Lucinda had been about, of course. But knowing her sister as she did, Miranda could hazard a fair guess. And she had no intention of participating in any discussion about errant earls and their remarkable reappearances.

Better to consign such happenings to story books of olde. For all their sakes.

Meanwhile, the viscount outstretched his meticulously pressed sleeve. "So it is, Miss Drayton. If you would do me the honor."

Miranda's smile came easier as Lord Hawthorne led her away from her troublesome sister and toward the dance floor.

She'd come to reserving the viscount the first set, so it was comforting to slip into their established routine.

"You are looking radiant this evening," he commented.

Whilst he needn't sound so surprised, Miranda beamed all the same. "And you, rather dashing."

She clasped his outstretched hand, and he swept her into the first spin.

Strong, faithful, dependable. Lord Hawthorne was truly all one could wish for in a match.

After their turn, Miranda stepped back into line. She smiled at the gentleman to her right as he took her hand for the next steps of the quadrille.

Throughout their set, her thoughts never strayed from Lord Hawthorne. Less chance of disturbing memories intruding that way. And if she felt a shiver of apprehension grace the back of her neck now and then, she sensibly attributed the sensation to a passing draft from the terrace doors.

Soon enough, she was back in the viscount's capable hands, and the world realigned itself accordingly.

"Would you care for a ride in my curricle on the morrow?" he asked. "I have some matters to see to in the morning but could come by afterwards. If you're amenable, of course."

Miranda blinked back her surprise.

Given his numerous duties pertaining to the family estates, the viscount rarely found time for the like. As such, their interactions to date had been confined to routs like the Cumberland's, the odd dinner party, and on very special occasions, the theatre.

Miranda dipped into a curtsy as the last notes of the quadrille faded away. "That would be delightful, my lord. I shall look forward to it."

Smiling, she took the viscount's arm for the walk back to the others.

James Stanton's reappearance wasn't so disconcerting, now she had a ride with the viscount to consider.

The path forward was set, and the designated route couldn't be clearer. Miranda knew where she was heading, and she wasn't about to let anything thwart her.

Wayward earls and their unexpected returns notwithstanding.

2

A Marked Man

With much rustling of taffeta, Lady Cumberland finally made way to greet a rowdy bunch of latecomers. James watched on, marveling at how the countess could maneuver at all in a skirt twice as wide as her hips. As it were, several guests had to awkwardly sidestep to avoid being swallowed whole in her wake.

He darted behind the young revelers, though he knew the reprieve was bound to prove fleeting.

Those blood-nosed matrons were trained to sniff out an unattached title from more than ten paces, hence he'd timed his arrival well after the receiving line had disbanded. Otherwise, he would've been swarmed the moment he stepped foot into the ballroom.

Now to avoid the inevitable reintroductions but a while longer...

Hugging the long wall of the gilded ballroom, James clocked two Turner's, a Lawrence—and if he wasn't entirely mistaken—an original Rembrandt, along the way. He then cast his eye over the assembled guests, all obligingly draped in their finest, and looking to have emptied their jewelry cases over their heads before venturing out for the evening.

But amongst the ostentatious display, one gem took precedence. Miss Miranda Drayton. The vision in pale muslin currently gliding across the floor on the arm of her noble swain.

James swiped a glass of claret from a passing footman's tray and dipped into an alcove directly in line with the dancers. Downing his drink, he winced, the wine doing little to ameliorate the bitter taste to his mouth.

Looking back, he easily set Miranda apart from the pretenders.

Time seemed to slow as she pirouetted, her midnight tresses all aglow under the hundred or so candles lighting her way. Then all too soon, she came to a stop, settling across from Hawthorne with a soft smile. A smile James remembered only too well.

His jaw tightened as he faced what had prompted his preemptive return to society, where only the senseless or desperate dared tread. The estimable Lord Hawthorne had finally decided on Miss Drayton as his viscountess—or so the odds in White's betting book favored.

James' take on the happy news differed markedly to the general consensus, however. Upon hearing the talk, he'd immediately gone off his dinner, then wondered at his adverse reaction. He hadn't sighted Miranda in years—for very good reason—so what right did he have to an opinion at all?

None whatsoever, many would surely argue.

Yet after no little reflection over more brandies than he cared to admit, he couldn't escape the fact. Hawthorne—upstanding and respectable fellow he may well be—wasn't at all right for Miranda. And seeing them dance together—their every step so measured, their stance so painstakingly *proper*—only cemented the notion. For all their simpering smiles, this was no love match. Any fool could see that. Which begged the question: Why was Miranda even considering Hawthorne in the first place? She'd always maintained that she wouldn't marry for anything less than complete devotion. And surely, she couldn't have altered that much in three years.

That left the worrying conclusion that she was being coerced in some way. And James found he couldn't rest until he discovered the truth, one way or the other. Miranda had saved him from a particularly dark place once, whether she appreciated it or not. Thus, he owed her the same courtesy, in the very least.

"James, old chap, I am surprised to find you here," said an amused voice, interrupting James' reverie. "Finally succumbed to the lure of the marriage mart, I see. Although, you won't get very far hiding here in the shrubbery."

James raised a brow as he turned to greet Lord Frederick Camden, his long-time friend. "I would hardly call it hiding, Freddy. Not when you happened upon me so readily. Besides, if I were truly bent on concealment, I would never be found. As you well know."

Freddy chuckled, tipping his imaginary hat in acknowledgment. "But what you fail to recall, dear chum, is that I already have all your favored hiding spots carefully catalogued for future reference right here." He tapped his temple in demonstration then waved to the potted fern to their left. "And even you must admit, this is woefully poor for your standards."

James raised his empty glass in salute.

Having met their first year at Eton, he and Freddy had quickly bonded over their shared propensity for mischief, not to mention their relief at escaping their overwhelmingly female environs back home.

Being an only child—stepsisters not included, of course—James considered Freddy more a brother than friend, and they'd remained close over the years. This despite their paths rarely crossing during the season, Freddy having two younger sisters to offload and James, an understandable aversion to ballrooms.

"How's the husband hunting going?" James asked, smiling at the pained look that crossed his friend's features in response.

"Tedious as ever," Freddy despaired. "Society's brimming with fops with little to recommend them. As such, I'm sure to reach my dotage before I see either of my sisters safely wed. Annabel has several admirers but is unwilling to play favorites. Because she enjoys leading the lot around by their cravats, I expect. And Sarah? Why, she's so deuced hard to read, I have no notion which young buck, if indeed any at all, has caught her eye. I've petitioned Mother to intervene, but she only laughs off my concerns, advising patience of all things. As if I have nothing better to do than squire the three of them about Town all season!"

James chuckled.

He didn't envy his friend in the least and was grateful he wasn't expected to do the same for his stepsisters, their mother, Muriel, being more than capable of seeing to that ambition herself.

"You know you adore all the rigmarole, Freddy," he said. "Otherwise, you'd refuse an invitation once in a while. Besides, your sisters' prospects cannot be that dire, them being attractive enough gels with modest dowries to boot."

"Ah, but that's where you're mistaken, dear chap," Freddy wisely intoned. "The ton's practically awash with pretty girls these days, you need only look."

James disregarded his friend's outstretched hand. He wasn't here for the scenery.

"Say, you're not interested in one of my sisters for yourself?" Freddy suggested with a disturbing jiggle to his brow. "That would be awfully convenient, and I'd be the first to welcome you into the family."

James ruefully shook his head.

A wife was the last thing he needed.

He could barely look after himself as it was.

"Sorry to disappoint, old chap. But as much as I adore your sisters and would be honored to call you brother in truth, I cannot see myself attached to either of them. Not even 'Pixie Pigtails'."

Freddy snorted, which sent his angelic curls flying. "Ho! If our Sarah ever heard you referring to her by that old moniker, my dear fellow, she would happily skewer you and probably me both by extension."

"Consider me duly warned, then," James retorted, happy to have avoided any awkwardness one might expect after dismissing one's friend's sisters out of hand.

In the companiable silence, James' attention drifted back to the dance floor.

Freddy followed his gaze. "If my charming sisters are not to your taste, then who's the lucky lass to have caught your eye this evening?"

James didn't respond.

Freddy was nothing but perceptive, though.

"Ho, ho, good luck to you there," he chortled after correctly ascertaining James' trajectory.

James turned, cutting his friend a deadly glare. Which only caused the blighter to laugh all the harder.

"Oh, don't get your cravat in such a twist, Stanton." Freddy was unrepentant. "I only find it ironic that you've set your sights on the one lady who's least likely to fall at your feet."

Now that *did* get James' back up. He'd certainly never received any complaints in the past. Not that he was after Miranda. At least, not in that sense.

Still, there was the principle of the thing.

"What makes you say that, *old chum*? Because the colonel is ever-so-subtly throwing her in Hawthorne's direction? For these past two years, I might add, and to little avail."

Freddy raised his brows. "Even so, Miss Drayton doesn't seem averse to the match now, does she?"

James frowned, refusing to concede his friend might have a valid point. But whilst Miranda's partiality for the viscount grated, the way she regarded Hawthorne paled in comparison to the look she gave James all those years before. As if he were all her most fanciful Christmas wishes wrapped in one massive bow.

Not that *that* had any bearing on the situation.

Hawthorne could well do with some competition, though. If only to prove his mettle.

"I wouldn't be discounting my suit quite yet," James found himself saying, choosing to ignore his friend's dubious expression in response.

Freddy didn't know the full story.

He and Miranda had been close once—a little too close than was strictly prudent, hence the subsequent need for distance—but close all the same. And one couldn't easily discount such feelings. Heaven knew, James had certainly tried.

"James, dearest, fancy meeting you here. In a *ballroom* of all places."

James turned to meet his godmother's arched look.

The Dowager Duchess of Winchester cut a regal figure, dressed in a billowing gown of green and gold silk. The monstrous creation she had perched on her head added to the overall effect, he supposed, but he couldn't help but pity the sacrificial peacock involved. Such was the high price of fashion.

Alongside the Dowager Duchess was her unassuming companion, Meg, and he bowed to kiss their proffered hands in turn.

"Godmother, and dearest Meg. What an absolute pleasure it is to see you both."

The Dowager Duchess tsked, swatting him aside. "Enough of that, my boy."

James grinned and went to introduce Freddy. But the baron had already taken himself off, the wily fellow.

"To what do we owe the unexpected pleasure?" his godmother asked next.

"Certainly not the refreshments." James scowled at his glass before handing the offending receptacle to a passing footman. He then returned to his godmother, being mindful to include Meg as he said, "But when one considers the company, why, I find it very much improved."

"Oh, pish!" the Dowager Duchess snorted. "Do spare us the pretty platitudes. Especially as the sentiment hasn't compelled you to visit any time recently, hmm?"

James shifted his weight.

His godmother was the only person in existence who could bring him to blush like a schoolboy.

She then turned to another sore subject, hardly enticing James to visit any time soon.

"And speaking of family, I see Lady Stanton and your youngest stepsister—Cecily, if I recall correctly—enjoying themselves by the Grecian column over there. Well, if 'enjoying' is the right word," she amended after taking in the Dowager Countess' expression.

His stepmother did indeed look unimpressed, which wasn't unusual.

James' lips tightened as he turned his back on the pair. "I appreciate the forewarning, Godmother. Wouldn't want to ruin the evening with an ambush."

"I don't think you can avoid the lady altogether, though," Meg said with a commiserating look. "She is family after all."

Signing a scrap of parchment didn't make someone family in James' book, but all he said was, "Just watch me, Meg," and flashed her an irreverent grin.

"Impertinent scamp." The Dowager Duchess reclaimed his attention with a sharp rap of her fan. "We have missed you dreadfully, though."

Ah, there it was. The surreptitious stab to the gut when one had just started to lower one's guard.

James fought a surge of guilt, the feeling never far from the surface where his godmother was concerned. Whilst she'd never directly challenged him on his sudden deflection, he suspected she knew it had something to do with Miranda. Reason enough for keeping his distance, despite his deep affection for the lady.

The time for evasion, however, was at an end.

"I see Lady Drayton and her daughters have also attended this evening," he said.

"Indeed." The Dowager Duchess gave a knowing look but proceeded as James intended, taking his arm in a firm grip. "Well then, my boy, lead on. As they say, there's no time like the present."

3

A Disgruntled Lady

Back with her mother and sister, Miranda thanked Lord Hawthorne for the dance. Unsurprisingly, Lord Sommerville and her father had already departed for the card room. The viscount went to join them, promising to return to escort her to supper.

Throughout the exchange, Lucinda shifted in place, managing to contain herself until the viscount was just clear of earshot. Then came the torrent.

"How was the dance? Did Lord Hawthorne have you completely transported? Any man worth his weight in salt should be light on his toes." Lucinda went still then, suddenly aghast by the thought. "Could you imagine it, Mira? A man incapable of the simplest country reel?"

Miranda hid a smile, thinking of many a worse trait in a future mate. Fortunately, the viscount could hold his own on the dance floor. Just another mark in his favor.

"Never fear, Lu," she said, "Lord Hawthorne executed the steps with his usual grace. And he must've been similarly impressed by my efforts, seeing he invited me for a ride in his curricle..."

Hearing Lucinda's peal in response, Miranda could only wonder. Whilst similarly pleased by the turn of events, she could hardly garner the same level of enthusiasm as her dear sister. Obviously, a personal deficiency on Miranda's part rather than having anything to do with the viscount per se.

"Now there's a precursor to proposal, if ever I heard one," said a dry voice on his approach.

Miranda turned, brightening to see the young solicitor Mr. Christopher Burton as he had his twin sister, Emily, by his side. She immediately moved forward to welcome the pair.

Lucinda held back. "Indisputably," she directed at the brother.

Miranda pressed Emily's hand in greeting, and they exchanged amused looks.

Friends since their respective debuts, she and Emily were more than accustomed to their respective siblings' squabbling. Appreciative even, if only for the entertainment they provided during the more trying events of the season. Therefore, neither were surprised when Christopher—or Kit, as he so preferred—was quick to retort.

"Honestly, Miss Lucinda, I wasn't being serious. Gentlemen invite ladies to the Park all the time, in case you were unaware. Lord Hawthorne probably desires some company whilst out exercising his cattle. Hardly something to write home about. No offense intended, Miss Drayton," he added as an aside.

Miranda smiled in return.

Kit only spoke the truth. The Park at fashionable hour was an event unto itself. But seeing the viscount rarely engaged in the pastime himself, his invitation *did* indicate a significant shift in their courtship. Not that she would be sharing that insight any time soon.

There was plenty enough speculation about her and the viscount as it was.

Meanwhile, Lucinda had turned to Kit in affront. Set to launch into a counter argument, one could only presume.

Fortunately for Kit, the Dowager Duchess and Meg were fast upon them. Unfortunately for Miranda, they'd brought James along with them, the latter looking far too sure of himself than surely warranted.

Her mother was quick to greet them. "Your Grace, Lord Stanton, and Mrs. Barlow. How lovely it is to see you all."

The Dowager Duchess clicked her tongue. "Heavens, Nora, no need for such formality. We are family, are we not?" She accepted a sisterly buss to her cheek then waved a hand in James' direction. "You remember my scamp of a godson, of course."

"Of course! It's an absolute pleasure, my lord," Lady Nora cooed, lifting her hand for James' ready kisses.

The skin on the back of Miranda's own hand twitched. Recoiling at the florid display, no doubt.

She stepped back as James loomed closer to be introduced to Emily and Kit.

Looking anywhere but at him, Miranda concentrated on her breathing.

Nothing could have prepared her for this moment, she realized, despite the numerous times she'd replayed this exact scenario in her head. Then to add to injury, James spoke, his all-too-familiar drawl darting shivers down her spine.

"You are looking well, Lady Drayton. In fact, you've hardly aged a day since we last met, which has been far too long by my reckoning."

"Likewise, my lord," Lady Nora responded in kind. "Why, we were only just saying how long it had been, weren't we girls?"

Miranda closed her eyes.

How pleased James would be by the revelation!

If only she could disappear beneath the floorboards. Or better yet, will him away again, thereby saving everyone the trouble.

"A neglect I plan to fully redress, madam," James vowed with such sincerity that Miranda turned to him in shock.

A patent mistake on her part. For James wasn't looking at her mother as one would reasonably expect. Instead, his honey-brown gaze was trained Miranda's way, shining with an intensity that seemed to swallow her whole.

Her breath hitched even as Lucinda asked, "Lord Stanton, do tell. How have you been amusing yourself these long years between visits?"

For once, Miranda was grateful for the interjection, and she tore her gaze away from James so she could slant her sister a quelling look. Not that it made an ounce of difference, Lucinda only having eyes for the rogue.

True to form, James responded lightly, saying, "Oh, this and the other," thereby leaving everyone to their own scandalous conclusions. He then addressed Miranda directly. "And how are you enjoying the evening, Miss Drayton?"

Despite her whole body going numb, Miranda somehow managed an airy, "Very well, my lord. And you?"

If he could act as if they were nothing but passing acquaintances, then so could she!

"I have found the evening only improves with each passing moment," he said, his lips tipping up in a grin. "Indeed, I would be most honored if you would partner me in the next set."

Good gracious, no!

Miranda felt herself pale as she looked down and glared at the vacant spot on her dance card. Whatever was she to do?

She turned to Lucinda, but her sister had already been claimed by a Mr. Buckworth so was of no help. Then for some obscure reason, her mother took it upon herself to accept in her stead.

"Miranda would be delighted. Wouldn't you, dearest?"

James' smile turned wry as Miranda could do little but air a stiff, "Of course."

At his outstretched sleeve, she reluctantly laid her hand atop, almost recoiling as the heat from his forearm seemed to burn right through her glove.

Wrestling her wayward response, she allowed James to sweep her toward the gathering dancers.

Hadn't she suffered enough, struggling to put the past behind her? Now, she not only had to face James after all this time, but *dance* with him at that. God knew the disaster that had befallen her the last time she'd been in his arms.

Reaching the dance floor, Miranda stepped back. But she could barely draw breath before the quartet picked up and James took her hand in readiness for the reel.

As they weaved between their fellow dancers, she risked a side glance and stiffened to find James watching her from the corner of his eye. He smiled, and her heart skittered in her chest.

She narrowed her gaze, not appreciating the feeling one iota.

How could he be so calm when she was anything but? Didn't he recall the circumstances when they last met?

Miranda didn't know whether to be insulted or relieved if that indeed was the case.

"Are we to go the entire set without speaking, then?" he asked.

James watched as Miranda struggled to form a reply.

Had her skin always looked so soft, iridescent even, in the candlelight, he wondered. And had her green-brown eyes always blazed with such passion? Although by the looks of it, she was considering serious bodily harm rather than a more pleasant kind of tussle. Still, he would take whatever she was offering over plain indifference.

"Of course not, my lord," she eventually said, pursing her rosy lips. "What do you wish to discuss?"

"Anything you like," he offered in return. "As I recall, we've never been in want of conversation before."

When she pressed her lips together, he suggested, "Tell me of your youngest siblings, then. How do they fare?"

Finally, he saw the makings of a smile.

Miranda had always held her siblings close. Good to know that hadn't changed at least.

"They're still irritating the colonel no end," she said, her eyes softening to a moss green. "Rebecca adamantly refuses to undertake any 'ladylike' pursuits, and Jonathan is...well...still Jonathan."

James chuckled softly.

The Drayton siblings had always been a boisterous lot, and he recalled the colonel's dismay at failing to contain the tribe whenever they were hell-bent on mayhem. No wonder he'd enjoyed holidaying with them so much, seeing how markedly they differed from his own family. And despite the strong bond they shared, they'd always made room, accepting James as one of their own. Miranda particularly.

"I expect you could never call the Drayton household dull," he remarked.

"Dull's not the first word that comes to mind, certainly." Miranda sent him an ironic look, and something indiscernible passed between them. A special something that caused James' heart to beat all the harder.

Then she blanketed her gaze once more.

Damn and blast!

Well, it was nice whilst it lasted, he supposed.

He'd expected some degree of awkwardness, but not this icy silence. Seemed his protracted absence had done more harm than he'd realized.

Of course, his leaving had been for the best. Whether Miranda had come to the same conclusion though, remained to be seen. The middle of a society ballroom didn't exactly lend itself to such confidences, however.

Time—that was what they needed. Some privacy wouldn't go astray, either. Unfortunately, to take a lady over your shoulder and abscond from the room was frowned upon. No matter how effectual, never mind honorable, the intention.

"May I call on you tomorrow?" he asked as the next best option.

She looked horrified by the suggestion. "You may do as you like. But if you happen to call, I will not be at home, I'm sorry to say."

Oddly enough, she didn't sound the least apologetic.

James couldn't leave it at that, of course. Miranda obviously wished to keep him at a distance.

Too bad he wasn't about to fall in line.

"That's a shame as I thought you might like to take a turn around the Park. Tomorrow's weather promises to be ideal for riding."

She seemed only the more irritated. "Indeed? Then, that *is* a shame, my lord. But surely, there must be someone, someplace, who'd be positively thrilled to accompany you."

James grinned.

She had pluck; he'd give her that.

"Undoubtably," he said. "But none who could even begin to compare."

She snorted. "Come now, that's doing it a little brown. Even for *you*."

He gave a mournful look. "You doubt my word? How that wounds me, my dear."

Her frown made clear exactly what she thought he could do with his 'word' and his personage besides. Still, James considered their verbal sparring an encouraging start.

When the reel called for him to pull her closer, he didn't shy away, confessing by her ear, "I've missed you, you know."

Her eyes shot to his, doubt evident in their glossy depths. So he delayed the release of her hand just a tad, hoping she could feel the truth to his words.

He certainly felt her quiver in response.

Despite the warning bells going off in his head, he relaxed, reveling in every glance, every touch, as they weaved back and forth in time with the music. Dancing with Miranda felt like the most natural thing in the world. An inherent danger in itself.

He couldn't seem to help himself though, sending her a heated look and almost missing a step to see her deepening blush.

How she would look draped across his silken sheets in that exact color. In *only* that color.

Now, where had that treacherous thought sprung up from?

From that part of his brain he kept securely locked away for the greater good, no doubt.

With his cravat suddenly felt too tight, he slowed his breathing, though it made scant difference. Then the dance came to a precipitous end.

Stepping back, Miranda mumbled her thanks.

He bowed, incapable of responding as everything in his head sounded pitifully trite.

Taking Miranda's arm for the short walk back to the others, he tried to ignore how carefully she held herself apart from him.

He wouldn't be discouraged.

No point in returning only to run at the first sign of difficulty.

Because he wasn't adept at doing just that?

James banished that taunting voice along with his errant thoughts.

He'd mishandled things. That wasn't up for contention. Mistakes weren't irredeemable, though. He need only explain to Miranda his entirely valid reasons for leaving, then he could work on the rest.

Besides, he wasn't going anywhere this time. And the sooner Miranda realized that the easier it would be for everyone.

4

The Escape

James was set upon by a swarm of determined mamas and their 'darling' daughters the moment they vacated the dance floor. Miranda left him to it, her only thought being escape.

She slipped away to the retiring room with her friend, Emily, in tow.

"Would you ease up?" Emily gasped as they made quick work of the hall. "Or is racing to the retiring room the newest fashion?"

"No, sorry, of course it's not," Miranda said, moderating her pace.

It wouldn't do to be seen flying down the corridor like common harridans. Even if the impulse was entirely justified.

How dare James say that he missed her! If he'd truly missed her, he wouldn't have left it so long.

Channeling calm, Miranda pushed open the door to the cozy sitting room Lady Cumberland had appointed to serve as the necessary. Relieved to find the space unoccupied, she bypassed the plush-looking settee facing the fireplace and began pacing the length of the carpet, too agitated to sit.

This continued for several breaths. Until a small—but determined—obstacle stepped into her path.

"Now that you have dragged me here," Emily said, her tone breaking no argument, "would you care to explain *what the blazes is going on?*"

On occasion, Miranda had heard Emily being cruelly dismissed as mouse-like. But she would dare anyone to make that connotation now.

She swallowed convulsively. "Why, whatever can you mean?"

Emily snorted. "Come now, in the time we've known each other—and I feel I know you better than most—I have never seen you so, well, *flustered.* And Lord Stanton. Why have you never mentioned him previously, hmm?"

Oh, for far too many reasons to recount.

Miranda turned her head slightly, thereby avoiding her friend's gaze. "What can I say? We saw each other occasionally—in our youth, you must understand—but I wouldn't have called us close."

Not as close as she would have liked, in any case.

"Pfft!" Emily scoffed. "I was there, standing right beside you during the introductions, if you recall. I saw the way he looked at you and how equally determined you were *not* to meet his gaze. And when he had the temerity to ask you to dance, why, you looked set to cast up your accounts right then and there!" She shook her head. "I will tell you this much, Mira. You and Lord Stanton are not *mere* acquaintances. Look how tense you are just discussing the man!"

Miranda ceased her fidgeting in an instant.

She didn't wish to speak of James. Not when she was still struggling to understand the churning emotions his return had wrought. But she knew she had to offer her friend something, lest Emily imagine something altogether worse.

Unbeknown to most, Emily was the secret authoress of the titillating serial, *Miss M's Mysteries*, which had recently taken the ton by storm. As such, her friend sought out drama as a matter of course. Though a fiasco eclipsing *that* Christmas, Miranda couldn't envisage.

"It's a small thing really," she ended up saying, waving her hand around for effect. "I may have inconvenienced the earl once, but it's long forgotten."

Emily immediately latched onto the very crux of her statement. "What do you mean exactly by 'inconvenienced'?"

Miranda felt her cheeks heat as she looked to the cupid-inspired wallpaper beyond her friend's head. "I may have attempted a kiss under the mistletoe at Rose Manor one Yuletide, but I was soon put to rights."

Now she'd revealed her shameful secret, she hoped that would be the end of it.

She'd never been fortuitous by nature, though.

"You didn't!" Emily gasped, momentarily stunned into silence. She then regarded Miranda closely. "So, he wasn't receptive then, to your, your...?"

Mercifully, she left the remainder unsaid. Nevertheless, Miranda felt ill having to relive the tale.

"He thought it all a lark," she said, attempting to laugh it off. "Chalked it down to excessive exuberance, it being the season and all. It was nothing, truly."

Emily didn't look so convinced. "But why haven't you mentioned this before, Mira? It's not as if Lord Stanton hasn't come up in conversation."

That was certainly true.

Being an unattached earl of considerable means, one could hardly avoid the talk that followed him everywhere. Where every reckless jaunt across the Park, ridiculously obscene wager, and not-so-discrete liaison with one of those voluptuous actresses from Covent Garden—and by all accounts, they were well-gifted in that particular arena—was embellished and rehashed throughout Mayfair in unadulterated delight.

Not that such conduct was uncommon amongst his set, which by no means excused his behavior. Hardly fair considering if a maiden so much as looked at a gentleman a second overlong she was scolded for being fast and banished to the country until she could be trusted to act with more decorum.

Shaking off her agitation, Miranda sighed. "It's not something one brings up in normal conversation. *Oh, you mean* that *fellow. The one I foolishly threw myself at when I was seven and ten!*"

Emily laughed. "You didn't have to put it quite so theatrically, my dear, but I do take your point." And yet, it seemed she couldn't let it rest. "So, the kiss. How was it?"

"Emily!" Miranda was mortified by the question. "It's not as if he kissed me back—not by a great degree, anyway. It was pretty much over before it began. And considering I found him quite happily engaged with a more practiced widow the next afternoon, I feel it's safe to say the kiss was rather forgettable. From his standpoint at least."

Miranda did her best not to see her friend's pitying look.

"Oh, Mira. Whatever will you do now?" she asked.

"I don't believe there's anything to do," Miranda returned smartly. "Now the awkward reunion is over, I expect nothing but polite, if not distant, interactions henceforth. It's not as if James is actively seeking my company, or vice versa."

If Emily looked skeptical, she didn't voice her doubts.

"He'll be too busy warding off the circling debutants to concern himself with me," Miranda insisted. "You'll see."

As they left the retiring room and returned to the ballroom, Miranda wasn't quite sure who she was trying most to convince.

Her friend or herself.

***

Several hours later, Miranda sank wearily into the well-sprung squabs of the family coach for the short journey home. A ride that would undoubtably take an hour given the post-ball congestion.

Her mother looked set to doze. There was time aplenty, so why not take advantage? Lucinda sat quietly by her side, staring into the inky darkness outside the window.

From the opposing seat, Miranda frowned.

Her sister was usually a fountain of talk at the end of an evening, her excitement about who was seen with whom—and sometimes more scintillatingly, who was seen without—knowing no bounds. Not this evening though, which was especially odd given certain developments.

Miranda briefly considered asking the matter, but as Lucinda would likely respond in kind, she let the impulse slide.

She had ample problems of her own to contend with.

Despite the disastrous start to the evening, Miranda had made a point of dancing every set like she would any other evening. Unfortunately, James had been of a similar mind, standing up with every available debutant from what Miranda could tell, and a few fawning dowagers besides.

Not that she was jealous. If James wished to be slavered all over like Mrs. Bell's latest fashion plate, that was entirely his prerogative. She was unused to seeing him, that was all, let alone bear witness as he romanced the better half of Mayfair in the space of one evening.

A rattling of the door saved Miranda from her thoughts and her eyes widened to see the colonel stepping into the carriage.

Her father rarely accompanied them home of an evening, preferring to stop by his club before making his own way back later.

Lady Nora bolted upright in her seat. "Why are you not at your club, sir?" she asked, looking naturally unsettled by her husband's break in habit.

"Not this evening, my dear, as I couldn't wait to share the glorious news!" Sir Richard's triumphant look was met by their arched glances. "The Duke of York—*the Commander-in-Chief himself*—made a point of commending me on my proposal. Not only that, but several peers vowed to give my bill due consideration when it's finally tabled at the end of the week."

Miranda joined in her family's congratulations.

Since resigning his commission, her father had turned his attention to the military's distribution channels. The lack of even the basic supplies was crippling their troops on the continent, he maintained, thereby threatening their continuing success against Napoleon. Now a vocal proponent of reform, his proposed rehaul of the current system was being presented at the House of Lords via Lord Sommerville for their esteemed peers' deliberation.

Miranda smiled, knowing how tirelessly her father had toiled to reach this point. "That's wondrous, Father. The more support you can garner beforehand, the greater likelihood your improvements will be adopted without too much rigmarole and delay."

"There's bound to be plenty of that, regardless. This *is* the peerage we are talking about," he returned with an ironic look. "But I hear it's been a successful evening all round. A curricle ride with Lord Hawthorne, I take it?"

At her nod, he palmed his thigh with a resounding slap. "Splendid! Then it shouldn't be long before we have further cause for celebration, eh my dear?"

Miranda somehow managed a murmur of agreement in return.

Her father then turned to the window. His thoughts already trained on the next stage of his campaign, no doubt.

Biting her lip, Miranda's thoughts returned to her own crusade. But how difficult it was to focus on the future when memories of James kept dragging her back into the past. A place she had no desire whatsoever to revisit, let alone dwell.

What she needed was for James to similarly take stock of the evening and decide he and society didn't suit after all, then disappear for another three years or so.

Now, that would be most obliging.

5

The Past – Rose Manor, Christmas Eve, 1809

Huddled beside the grandfather clock in her aunt's drafty hallway at a quarter to midnight, Miranda started to question her sanity. Who in their right mind would risk possible hypothermia—on Christmas Eve, no less—just for the sake of a kiss?

But then, this wasn't to be any old kiss. This was to be her first. And what could be grander than having your very first kiss under the mistletoe with the person you adored most in the world?

James Stanton.

Just mouthing his name sent a course of shivers through her body.

From the moment she'd first sighted him as a surly ten-year-old boy, the wounded look in his eyes had tugged at her heartstrings. As time went on, his grief over his sire's passing had lessened as their friendship grew, and so too had her affections blossomed. And now that Miranda was on the verge of making her debut, and James quite the man about town, her feelings had taken on a new dimension that refused to be ignored.

In short, she'd turned into one of those pitiful creatures who couldn't go a minute without thinking of their beloved. Where he was, what he was doing, and *who* he was doing it with. Indeed, the whole sorry business was sending her half-crazed. So much so, she feared she would end up in Bedlam if she didn't do something about it.

That was when she'd decided to act. Soon they'd all be returning to London, and Miranda found she couldn't leave without knowing whether James felt the same. And surely, he must. For the alternative was inconceivable.

The grandfather clock at her back suddenly struck twelve.

Miranda placed a hand against her beating chest and peered around the clock to the front door, wondering wherever he could be.

James had decamped for Alton's tavern straight after supper, favoring an ale with the local lads over the perfectly amiable game of charades her Aunt Bethel had organized in the front parlor.

But that was hours ago, and if he didn't return soon, Miranda feared she'd lose her nerve, or worse: End up as a frozen monument to her foolishness.

Finally, she heard the scrape of the lock. Turning her head, she could just make out his heavily cloaked figure in the gloom. James muttered to himself as he brushed the snow from his broad shoulders. Then he removed his coat and started up the hall.

Ducking back into the shadows, she took a deep breath.

This was it. The moment of reckoning.

She stepped out from behind the clock with an air of confidence she wasn't even close to achieving.

James stopped two feet shy of her, directly beneath the kissing bough conveniently dangling from the archway overhead.

"What the devil," he exclaimed, his eyes widening in shock. "Miranda? Talk about an apoplexy! Whyever are you not abed?" He looked to the hallway beyond as if expecting the answer to leap from the shadows. "It's surely Christmas morn by now."

"So, it is," Miranda returned in a rush. And before she could think, she reached her hands to his shoulders and whispered, "Merry Christmas, James," then pressed her mouth against his frost-bitten lips.

He stiffened at the contact, and she counted three ticks of the clock before he moved. Then, incredibly, he took control, and my, wasn't it worth the wait.

Shivering, she sank deeper into his embrace, wanting closer. Wanting his all. His woolen jacket was soft to touch, he smelt faintly of tobacco and tasted of what she assumed to be ale. And he was warm. So very, very warm.

She sighed as a delicious tingly feeling began to traverse her whole body. Even her toes were curling in delight. She reached up to run her fingertips through the silky strands at his nape.

Still, it wasn't nearly enough.

James groaned as if pained, his hands briefly tightening at her waist before, abruptly, they were gone.

"Enough!" he rasped, dragging his hand through his hair as if to rid himself of her touch. "Have some care, Miranda. We're well past the age for such games, don't you think?"

Miranda was too stunned to speak.

She'd never seen James so stern, let alone have him address her so coldly. Not quite the falling to his knees to profess his undying love that she'd envisioned more than once, to her utmost shame.

He was mistaken, however. This was no lark.

It was anything but.

"But I'm not...That's to say..." She paused to draw in a much-needed breath. "You don't seem to—"

He brought a finger to her lips, silencing her. "*Now* I understand. Too many dips into the wassail, I expect." He removed his finger to tweak her nose. "You'll have a dev— terrible headache on the morrow, Mira dear. But as they say, we live and learn. Now, off to bed with you." He made a shooing motion. "You know how the Dowager Duchess gets if we're late to Christmas services."

"But James," Miranda protested, needing him to understand. "You must allow me—"

"Uh-uh." He cut her off again, shaking his finger like she was some unruly child. "If your father were to catch wind of this, he'd have me straight to the firing squad, quick march."

The prospect seemed to amuse him, but Miranda couldn't return his smile. Numb as she was, she doubted she could move her lips even if she tried. So she nodded and turned slowly toward the stairs, picking up her pace on the ascent.

What an absolute nightmare!

James didn't want her, clearly. Indeed, he seemed mighty keen to see the back of her, which told Miranda all she needed to know.

He still saw her as a child. His friend, nothing more.

She cleared the top of the staircase and hurried toward her bedchamber, not looking to see if he followed lest he witness her mortification.

Safely inside her room, she leaned her forehead against the closed door.

What had she been thinking, accosting James in the hallway like, like...*a common strumpet?* No wonder he'd withdrawn in disgust.

She stalked across the room, untying her dressing gown and flinging it away. Clambering onto the bed, she considered herself fortunate that James thought her inebriated. At least then he'd never suspect her true feelings, nor realize he'd crushed all her hopes and dreams in one fell swoop.

Lying back, she burrowed under the coverlet and squeezed her eyes shut.

If only she could blot the entire incident out.

But nothing could stem the tears as she mourned all the things that could never be.

***

The very next day

Seated at her aunt's lavishly decorated dining table, Miranda laid down her fork, her appetite nonexistent.

Christmas Day. Mayhap the only day of the whole calendar year where one couldn't feign a headache so to avoid a certain someone. A fact she should've considered before embarking on her whatever-was-she-thinking gambit the previous evening.

Such was the benefit of hindsight.

In saying that, said evasion had been remarkably easy to accomplish. Miranda had barely laid eyes on James all day, let alone exchanged more than two words with him. It had helped, of course, him electing to sit at the opposite end of the pew for Christmas services, then three places along for her aunt's festive feast, though he could hardly be credited with the table arrangements.

She should be happy, having avoided the embarrassment of a confrontation. And she may well have been if it wasn't for Lady Edwina, the neighboring squire's widowed daughter who'd been placed beside James for dinner.

Miranda stiffened as Lady Edwina trilled yet another laugh.

James' exchanges with the merry widow had only become more outrageous with each passing course; their brazen flirting cause enough to turn any discernable person off their stuffed pheasant and parsnips, never mind how succulent the dish.

Was it any wonder James hadn't gone out of his way to challenge Miranda on her behavior the previous evening? He had more pressing concerns. Namely, the voluptuous temptress blatantly brushing against his hand as he passed her the peas.

Miranda pushed aside her plate and reached for her wineglass.

Not long now, she assured herself.

The footmen were removing the last remnants of the meat course, making way for the platters of cheese, sugar plums, and thick slices of Mrs. Pott's top-heavy plum pudding.

Toying with her dessert, Miranda counted the minutes until her aunt finally rose from her seat and declared there was to be no port that evening. Instead, the gentlemen were expected to join the ladies in the drawing room for eggnog and a singsong.

Miranda had never been less enthused for the post-feast caroling, usually her favorite Yuletide tradition. She trailed behind the other guests and formulated an excuse to retire early.

In the parlor, Aunt Bethel had taken her customary position beside Meg on the pianoforte, music sheets at the ready. The guests were gathering around, chatting gaily amongst themselves as several footmen in waistcoats of crimson and gold distributed generously filled beakers.

Only one person was missing.

Miranda slipped back into the hall and marched over to the coat rack.

If James wasn't compelled to stay and pretend all was holy and bright, then neither would she!

She grabbed her coat and wrapped her woolen scarf around her neck, then headed out the front door.

The garden positively shimmered after the recent snow, but she didn't pause to appreciate the vista. Instead, she tugged her coat closer and set down the side path at a brisk pace.

Trudging through the snow, she tramped out her frustration. Which was all well and good until a breathy '*Dear heavens!*' had her pulling short of the rose arbor.

Although she knew she'd live to regret it, she moved forward, bringing the entangled couple into full view.

What arbor provided adequate cover in the dead of winter at any rate?

James stood with his back to her, his head bowed as he suckled Lady Edwina's neck, to which his lover's response could be described as nothing short of ecstasy.

Miranda staggered backward.

James wasn't enamored with *her*. Why would he be when he had women like Lady Edwina at his disposal? How foolish to think she could even begin to compare with the like.

Fighting back tears, Miranda hastened to her room, where she spent the dwindling hours at her window box, watching the sun set on what had to be the worst day of her life.

Never again, she vowed. Never would she allow herself to be blinded by emotion.

She'd thought James loved her as she did him. Obviously, she'd succumbed to a bad case of wishful thinking.

She should probably thank him, having learned an important lesson. Her judgment was faulty and couldn't be trusted. Now aware of her failing, she would be more circumspect in future. She certainly never wished to experience the like ever again!

And when James saw her next, he'd barely even recognize her, how altered she would be.

6

The Present - Drayton House, 1813

Miranda woke with a start and shivered to find her skin clammy with sweat. She nestled further beneath the blankets to escape the morning chill.

It was early still, the hawkers touting their wares in the streets below with enough gusto to shatter windowpanes.

Miranda wasn't so keen to start the day, however. She'd spent the better part of the night reliving nightmares she'd thought long put to rest. She was tempted to lay back and shut her eyes to the world, but that would be self-indulgent. So she tossed off her bedclothes and headed for the washstand.

Filling the basin from the jug positioned alongside, she splashed handfuls of the ice-cold water onto her cheeks.

She glanced up and met her troubled gaze in the looking glass.

How ragged she looked. And all because James Stanton deigned to show his face in society.

Well, it wouldn't do! The fool girl who'd spent her waking moments clambering for every crumb of his attention was long gone.

What did it matter where James was, or even what he did? He'd be gone again soon enough anyway.

With her mind finally sorted, Miranda rang for her maid. Abigail appeared soon after, and in no time at all, Miranda was primmed and primed, ready to face whatever the day chose to throw at her.

First things first: breakfast.

She descended the stairs and headed to the dining room, finding her father in his usual seat at the head of the table.

Her proffered greeting was answered by grunt, the colonel fully engrossed in the newssheet he was reading.

Well used to her father's unique conversation style, Miranda took no offense. She turned to the sideboard and selected a helping of coddled eggs and a slice of toast then took her seat at the table.

Having little appetite, she slid her eggs from one side of the plate to the other, only to be startled when the colonel suddenly lowered his paper.

"Eat up, my girl. Why, you look positively peaked this morning! And you must be at your best when Lord Hawthorne comes a-calling. You haven't forgotten the day's outing, surely."

"Of course not, Father, I'm entirely looking forward to the ride," Miranda returned smartly, making a point of picking up her fork and bringing it to her mouth even though her eggs had congealed into something completely unpalatable.

The colonel grunted. "As well you should. The viscount's doing you a great service by taking you up in his curricle, which only goes to prove our campaign's finally making inroads. As such, we cannot afford to falter at the first hurdle and lose our advantage."

Miranda had to smile.

She could imagine her father similarly rallying his troops before sending them off into battle.

"I take you meaning, sir, and I can assure you, I'm more than equipped to meet any challenge put to me."

"That goes without saying. You are my daughter, after all," the colonel declared with a nod. He waved to her dish before returning to his own plate of kippers and eggs.

Miranda looked to the table, but instead of picking up her fork, she went for the tea pot, pausing mid-action at the sound of a disturbance in the hall.

The colonel placed down his cutlery just as his youngest progenies burst into the room.

"Victory is mine!" Jonathan declared smugly over his shoulder to where Rebecca was scurrying in after him.

Becca blew the hair from her face and looked up, her expression turning to horror once spying their father.

Miranda could only empathize as she too braced for impact.

"Rebecca, Jonathan," the colonel addressed them in carefully measured tones, "is that any way to enter a room?"

"No, sir. Sorry, sir," they said, their eyes downcast as they moved to their designated seats at the table.

"Pray endeavor to curb such behavior in future, then," he continued. "We live in civilized times, do we not? Therefore, I expect decorum to be upheld at all times. Understood?"

"Yes, sir," they chorused.

The colonel stood and gathered his broadsheet, tucking it under his arm as he made for the door. Before quitting the room entirely, he turned back to Miranda. "I expect a full report upon your return."

Miranda nodded, unsurprised by the directive.

Silence ensued as they watched him leave.

"*Sheesh*," Jonathan sounded as soon as the coast was clear. He turned to Miranda with a grin. "It appears our dear colonel got out of the wrong side of the bed this morning. If his bed even has a *right* side. Now you understand why I avoid these early starts, Mira. Despite my awakening in a state of near starvation every morn."

Miranda shook her head. "You're perpetually hungry, Jonathan, no matter the time of day, and you should be grateful having escaped with only a scolding. Whatever were you both thinking," she said, turning toward her sister, "to invite Father's wrath like that?"

Jonathan leaped to his feet. "I cannot speak for Becca, but as for myself, I was thinking of my stomach, of course!" He picked up a plate and set about ladening it with ham, chopped liver, coddled eggs, and several slices of thickly buttered toast.

Miranda could only wonder where he put it all.

Bemused, she turned back to Rebecca. "And what are your plans for the day, dearest?"

"I thought to try this new pastry recipe," Becca said, her cheeks coloring in her excitement. "Aunt Bethel sent over this cookery book, and it's entirely in French! The best *pâtissiers* all hail from Paris you know."

Miranda's smile widened.

Whilst her youngest sister despaired at being unable to master any of the 'feminine arts,' she'd somehow developed a talent for baking, much to their father's consternation. But Miranda couldn't see any harm in the hobby, especially when it gave her youngest sister such joy.

"Whatever you bake is bound to be delicious, Becca," she said, "and I'll be the first in line for the tasting."

Jonathan planted his plate on the table and smirked. "Too late, sis. I already have first claim. My prize winnings, eh, Becca?"

"I'm sure there will be plenty enough for everyone," Rebecca said, ever the peacemaker.

The conversation then turned to pastry fillings—Jonathan insisting jam topped custard in both taste and texture—and Miranda smiled to find nothing had changed.

The world hadn't shifted, or crumbled, or completely gone to ground. James' reappearance meant little in the grand scheme of things.

Honestly, she didn't know why she'd been so worried.

***

Some hours later, Miranda was seated beside her mother in the front parlor quietly minding her embroidery when her sister suddenly spoke up from her seat opposite. "Whatever could be the matter, Mira?"

Miranda slowly raised head and countered. "Why nothing at all, Lucinda. Why do you ask?"

Lucinda's look turned wry. "I don't know. Perhaps it has something to do with the way you're attacking your needlepoint with such vigor?"

Miranda briefly considered the monstrosity on her lap before tossing it aside. "I find myself anxiously awaiting the viscount, that is all."

Her sister nodded. "That would explain it. Bracing yourself for a tedious afternoon, I expect. Even you must admit, whilst Lord Hawthorne may be perfectly fine to look at and all, he's a bit of a dullard."

Miranda's jaw dropped.

This coming from the same sister who'd waxed lyrical about the viscount's dancing prowess only the previous evening?

"Lucinda!" Their mother paused from her tambouring to chide. "Lord Hawthorne isn't dull. He's simply, simply..." She tapered off, looking to Miranda in entreaty.

"Circumspect?" Miranda helpfully supplied.

"Precisely! Not dull but dutiful, and mindful of his responsibilities. In any case, having a dull husband would be the least of one's concerns, I would think," their mother concluded, leveling a frown Lucinda's way.

Miranda found herself in full agreement. One wouldn't suffer any unfortunate surprises then.

Not that the viscount was dull, as they'd already established.

But before she could belittle the point, their butler, Wilkins, appeared in the doorway. "His Lordship, Viscount Hawthorne."

As they went to rise, Lucinda murmured, "He's perfectly punctual, too. Shame that's not on my list."

"Mayhap it should be," Miranda hissed back.

Having devised her all-important List of Husband Attributes early in the season, it was all Lucinda could talk about, and heaven help the poor gentleman who fell short of her exacting requirements. But if a little staid was the worst trait she'd attributed to the viscount, Miranda counted herself lucky.

Turning to Lord Hawthorne, she was immediately taken aback. How well-turned out he looked in his riding gear!

Her unease returned with a vengeance, which was most odd.

She'd never been nervous in his presence before.

Thankfully, her mother was under no such hindrance, and she greeted the viscount with a smile. "Lord Hawthorne, good afternoon. I hope your trip across Town was pleasant."

"Good day, ladies," the viscount returned in his dulcet tones. "I faced no impediments on the ride over, I'm pleased to report."

"You didn't encounter any overturned apple carts in the street, then? Or some young buck losing control of his cattle?" Lucinda enquired, all innocence.

The viscount frowned. "Er, no, not at all."

"That's all right then," Lucinda went on to say brightly, "albeit a trifle *dull*, if you ask me."

"Sounds perfectly fortunate to me," Miranda cut in, shooting her sister a warning look as she stepped toward the viscount.

She'd be wise to expedite their departure given her sister's contrary mood.

Meanwhile, Lady Nora moved toward the bell. "Would you care for some tea, my lord? I'm about to call for a fresh pot."

"I'm sure Lord Hawthorne is eager to set off," Miranda said, directing a smile at the viscount to soften her sudden bluntness.

If they sat down to tea, they might never depart. Her mother could easily while the whole afternoon away over a pot when in the comfort of her own parlor.

"Indeed, that I am, Miss Drayton," Lord Hawthorne seconded, extending Miranda his arm. "My horses await us as we speak." He turned his conciliating smile back to her mother. "However, I expect to return for another visit soon, all things proceeding as expected."

"That would be lovely." Lady Nora nodded approvingly. "Pray enjoy the ride but do be careful. The traffic these days is atrocious."

Miranda's cheeks heated, but the viscount only smiled as he said, "I'll ensure to return your daughter safe and whole."

The farewells couldn't come quickly enough for Miranda, and she was relieved to finally clear the house with Lord Hawthorne intact.

7

A Fine Day for a Ride

Miranda accepted the viscount's hand as he assisted her into the curricle. They must've made a striking pair attired as they were in blue of a similar hue. Something Lucinda couldn't fail to appreciate from her position pressed against the front bay window, she didn't doubt.

If Lord Hawthorne noticed their curious onlooker, however, he was too well-mannered to comment.

He took his seat beside her and picked up the reins. "Blue suits you admirably."

Smiling wryly, Miranda thanked him for the compliment.

With a click of the tongue, Lord Hawthorne launched his pair of elegant grays into Grosvenor Street.

Breathing deeply, Miranda turned her face to the sun. She was all at once glad for the outing, the weather much too pleasant to spend ruminating indoors In fact, it was a day where all one's troubles seemed to catch on the breeze and float far, far away.

"It's a fine day for a ride, wouldn't you agree, my lord?" she said.

"Indeed, it is," the viscount agreed, eying her askance.

Their eyes caught for a moment and Miranda dropped her gaze to his hands.

Watching how expertly he managed the afternoon traffic, she reminded herself how secure her future would be in those hands.

Glancing back up, Miranda found they were already passing through Grosvenor Gate. Lord Hawthorne eased the horses to a walk, and she looked about in interest.

Hyde Park was teeming with people. There were many fine gentlemen on horseback, their steeds' well-brushed coats gleaming in the afternoon sun. Ladies in every shade of muslin and silk imaginable completed the pretty picture, either seated in open carriages like the viscount and herself or promenading the vast network of pathways on the arms of their attentive beaus.

A loud shout caught Miranda's attention, and she turned just as a couple of youths leaped straight into the Serpentine, boots and all.

"The Park is never dull, is it?" she said in amusement.

"Indeed."

Miranda hid a smile.

It seemed dips in the Serpentine weren't to be part of her future, judging by the viscount's frown. Not that it signified.

Whilst she did swim and quite happened to enjoy it, the last time she'd so partaken was at Rose Manor, and then...

Well, she wasn't dwelling on *then* anymore.

Dispensing with her wandering thoughts, she turned to the viscount.

"I believe my mother has the right of it," he was saying. "Where many a reputation is made, or indeed lost, in this very park."

Miranda nodded. For where would one be without their reputation?

"And how is Lady Sommerville? Improved with the milder weather, I trust?"

Lady Sommerville suffered from a detracting illness, which curtailed her attendance at most events of the season. But she more than compensated for her absence by hosting a lively soirée at home every Wednesday evening.

"Mother is traveling as well as can be expected," Lord Hawthorne said after some reflection. "She stoically refuses to dwell on her malady, and rightfully so. One in her position cannot afford to show any weakness, after all."

An understandable notion. The obligation to keep up appearances may be arduous, but it seemed to hold up the very fabric that was society. And Lady Sommerville held herself very well considering the challenges she faced. All of which made the viscount's loyalty to his family the more admirable.

"The earl and countess must appreciate your devotion, and will surely feel the loss upon your marriage," she said.

He seemed perplexed by her statement. "But nothing would change in that regard, Miss Drayton, as the future viscountess will be installed at Sommerville House, of course."

"Of course," Miranda echoed, biting back her surprise.

Whilst Lord Hawthorne spent most of his time in Town, she'd assumed that once wed, they'd make one of the family's estates dotting the country's southwest their home. At least, when Parliament wasn't in session.

"Your mother would certainly welcome your future wife's assistance then, with house management and the like?"

"She has all that well in hand. I fear Mother would find it difficult releasing the reins, so to speak, and frankly, who would blame her? Sommerville House is her sole purpose now her children are grown, and it would be unfair to take that away from her."

Miranda was miffed that he would think her so insensitive. Still, life as his viscountess was sounding more ornamental than practical by the minute. But she couldn't let that deter her.

She would just find something to occupy her time. Charitable endeavors, and the like. Then there'd be children, God willing.

At the sound of approaching hooves, an ominous shiver passed through Miranda. With good cause as she soon discovered.

James had reined in his horse by the curricle with his good friend Lord Camden pulling up alongside.

"Good day, Hawthorne, Miss Drayton," James said, flashing a toothy grin.

Miranda frowned, wondering what he could be so pleased about.

Hopefully whatever it was would soon have him on his way again.

"Stanton, Camden." Lord Hawthorne acknowledged them stiffly, slowing the horses to a crawl.

Lord Camden tipped his hat whilst James only continued his infernal smiling.

Feeling not the least amused by comparison, Miranda was loath to admit that they made a dashing pair, each so comfortable in their seats.

James looked to be the better horseman though, he and his magnificent steed moving as one.

An unexpected—and wholly unwarranted—wave of longing suddenly hit Miranda in the solar plexus. Quashing the sensation, she focused on Lord Camden, the least disturbing of the duo.

James continued in a jovial vein. "What a capital afternoon! Sunshine and good company make the best bedfellows, don't you think?"

Miranda left the inane comment well alone, leaving Lord Hawthorne to respond with a succinct, "Indeed."

With that, the viscount made it clear he had no desire whatsoever to prolong the exchange.

Not that James appeared concerned by his lackluster reception as he turned his molten gaze her way.

Well, Miranda *assumed* he was looking at her, seeing that side of her face was suddenly ablaze with a prickling heat. She wasn't about to turn to verify it, though.

"And Miss Drayton? How are you fairing this fine day?" he asked, all but confirming her suspicions anyway.

She flicked him a sour look, though she kept her words unfailingly polite. "Very well, my lord," she said, turning back to the baron. "And how are you finding the season, Lord Camden?"

"Exceedingly well, Miss Drayton," Freddy returned congenially. "With so many amusements to be had, my mother, sisters, and I could never claim to suffer from the ennui that seems to plague the ton. We are especially looking forward to your aunt's house party next week, never having the pleasure of an invite before."

Miranda tensed.

Of course, the Camden's acceptance did not necessarily mean James would follow suit. He certainly had never attended any of her aunt's house parties in the past, despite faithfully receiving an invitation every year. Furthermore, if he suddenly found space in his busy schedule, he would hardly refrain from pronouncing it to all and sundry, if only to vex certain people.

"You are sure to have a delightful time, Lord Camden," she said, releasing the tight hold on her breath. "Not only is Rose Manor happily situated in the Hampshire hills, but my aunt's cook makes the most delectable cinnamon scrolls imaginable."

Lord Camden chuckled good naturedly as he slid his companion a speaking look. "I've heard all about those infamous delights from my dear friend here, and so I'm counting the days in anticipation."

James took the mantle from his friend. "Ah, Mrs. Pott's famed scrolls. I shall never forget my first taste as a lad. Utterly spoiled me for all other treats, let me assure you."

Miranda almost smiled, but that would've only encouraged him.

It seemed James had altered little in the ensuing years. But if he expected to slip back into their old camaraderie as if nothing had changed, he would soon be disappointed.

Life had moved on. More importantly, *she'd* moved on. And all for the better.

James absently patted his bay mare's neck as he struggled to reconcile the woman before him with the Miranda he so fondly remembered. Holding herself so rigidly, and with her expression so grim, she seemed a world away from that carefree girl of years gone by.

That Miranda wouldn't sit passively and take in the sights on a day like today. She'd be raring to be let down from the carriage so she could explore the meadow for herself, laughing gaily all the while. She always seemed happiest when out of doors.

But seated there beside Hawthorne, she only looked miserable, where James' best efforts hadn't managed to coax out even a hint of a smile.

He had to resist the sudden urge to steal her away. Away from Hawthorne for starters, the viscount putting a dampener on anyone unfortunate to be within spitting distance.

How could anyone be content stuck in a curricle with that dull stick?

The breeze picked up then, catching a wisp of Miranda's ebony locks and playing it against her neck.

James swallowed, it being all he could do *not* to whisk her up on his mount and find them a shady spot. Then he could sweep those luscious tresses aside and replace them with his lips, turning her frowns into whimpers of delight.

He repositioned himself in his saddle, and his horse sounded her disapproval. He almost snorted right along with her.

He'd been back—what, all of two days?—and he was already inundated with improper thoughts. The very thoughts that necessitated his leaving in the first place. And their dance the previous evening hadn't helped matters. Now he had absolute proof. He hadn't imagined how perfectly Miranda fit in his arms back then. If anything, his memory had been severely defective. Which was fortunate else he mightn't have been able to stay away for as long as he had.

James looked back at the viscount and scowled.

Hawthorne had no idea how good he had it. He acted as if he fully expected the colonel to gift Miranda on a silver platter whenever he got around to the asking. And from James' knowledge of the colonel that probably wasn't too far off the mark.

But Miranda wasn't a piece of property to be palmed off to the first bidder, and Hawthorne a fool for not realizing her worth.

Hawthorne glared back at him, so James raised a brow just to irritate the dolt further. He wasn't going anywhere, and he didn't care a whit if the blasted fellow knew it.

"I am sure you have important business to attend to, Stanton. Pray, do not let us keep you," Hawthorne said.

His tone was impressive for its sheer dismissiveness. Still, James took great pleasure in refusing to take the hint. "*Au contraire*, Hawthorne, I've no pressing concerns at present. How 'bout you, Freddy?"

Freddy thought for a moment. "Nothing that immediately springs to mind."

James held back a laugh.

He could always count on dear Freddy to have his back.

Miranda looked only the more uncomfortable the longer they tarried, however.

"The day marches on, though, so we best be off," he conceded for her sake. "Have a pleasant ride, Hawthorne. Miss Drayton."

He took Hawthorne's dour expression in response as a personal triumph. And with one last lingering look Miranda's way, James turned his horse toward the green, challenging Freddy to a race as he was suddenly in need of the exertion.

8

The Inquisition

After bidding his farewells, Lord Hawthorne steered his curricle back down the drive.

Watching him leave, Miranda released her breath.

The ride home had been riddled with tension. For how on earth was she to answer him? She couldn't account for James' appearance at the Park, nor explain his inclination to linger. Besides, didn't the viscount realize? She didn't want to think of James, let alone discuss the fellow.

Walking into the house, Miranda thanked Wilkins as he took her bonnet and pelisse. She started up the hall, her step faltering when Lucinda materialized from the shadows.

"There you are, Mira," Lucinda said. "How was the ride? Tell me all, in meticulous detail."

Miranda laughed despite herself.

One couldn't be in the doldrums long with her sister in the vicinity.

"Can we at least repair to the parlor first?" she asked, setting off in that direction.

Lucinda grumbled from behind her. "If you insist."

Lady Nora raised her head as they entered the room. "Did you enjoy the outing, my dear?"

Miranda kissed her mother on the cheek, then resumed her seat on the chaise. "Yes, we had a pleasant ride. With the sun out, and a refreshing breeze drifting off the Serpentine, one couldn't ask for a finer day."

Lucinda snorted, landing heavily on the settee across from them. "Enough of the weather! What of Lord Hawthorne himself?"

Miranda chose her next words with care. "The viscount was gracious as ever, and we did enjoy a nice coze about his family."

Lucinda clasped her hands together. "Now, that's more like it! Such talk suggests Lord Hawthorne is preparing you for the next phase."

Considering her sister's current preoccupation, 'the next phase' could only mean the altar. A trifle presumptuous considering she and the viscount didn't exactly depart on the best of terms.

"And did you meet anyone of note?" her mother asked.

"Certainly," Miranda said. "It seemed half of Mayfair was out of doors this afternoon. Including Lord Stanton and Lord Camden, who pulled up to exchange pleasantries."

Miranda saw no point in concealing the fact. Her mother was likely to hear of the encounter in any case. Such was the way of the ton.

"Oh!" Lucinda had scooted so far to the edge of her seat, she looked liable to fall off at any moment. "Lord Camden's rather dashing, is he not? And the way he escorts his mother and sisters all about Town—willingly, mind you—attests to his affability, don't you think?"

Happy to keep the conversation confined to the baron, Miranda was quick to respond. "You'll be pleased to hear that the Camdens will be joining us at Rose Manor next week, then."

Lucinda was absolutely delighted by the news, considering her squeal. "You don't say! That means James must have accepted, too. What a merry time we'll all have!"

Miranda fought back a shudder as Lucinda took on a mischievous look.

"You know, if James weren't so old, and practically a brother to us and all, I would seriously consider him for a husband myself."

To say Miranda was shocked by her sister's declaration didn't quite cover it. "James isn't decrepit, Lucinda. He cannot be much older than Lord Camden, in fact."

As if she didn't know James' age down to the approximate timing of his birth.

"Not too old for you maybe," Lucinda allowed with a grin. "In fact, I would suggest him for yourself if you weren't so fixated on the viscount. For myself though, I require a husband closer to my age than the grave to keep pace with me. Otherwise, I'd be bored within a sennight."

Their mother gasped. "How shocking, Lucinda! As if a husband would be concerned with his wife's entertainment.

He'd have far more important things within which to occupy his time, let me assure you."

"The right husband would ensure his wife's happiness," Lucinda insisted. "Make it his mission, I would think. Therefore, it's imperative to choose wisely or else risk a lifetime of misery. I'm certainly not willing to settle, are *you*?" She directed the question to Miranda.

Miranda squirmed under her leveled stare. "Of course not. But don't you think this discussion is redundant? You know Father intends me for Lord Hawthorne."

"Be that as it may, Miranda dear, this is *your* future we're discussing," her mother said, "so ultimately, the decision must lie with you. I would loathe for you to regret your choice." *Like me* was the unspoken implication.

Miranda swallowed, unsure where all this concern had arisen from.

Her mother hadn't voiced doubts about the viscount before. In fact, she'd seemed quite happy to let the courtship run its predestined course, her actions earlier this afternoon being a case in point.

"I haven't taken the decision lightly, Mama. Marriage is until death and all. Lord Hawthorne is the man for me."

"As long as you're certain, my dear," she said, patting Miranda on the arm and returning to her tambouring.

Miranda sank back into the cushions.

How could the day have turned so abruptly?

Bad enough to encounter James a second time, but for her family to start questioning her judgement as well?

Yes, she'd made a terrible mistake once. But she'd learned her lesson and learned it well, where every decision she'd made thereafter had been well considered. From *every* conceivable angle.

Lord Hawthorne may be the colonel's choice initially, but Miranda couldn't fault her father's reasoning. The viscount was her perfect accompaniment in every way. He didn't have her all tied up in knots for starters, and she could always think clearly in his calm, reassuring presence. All prime indicators that she was on the right path, her mother's and sister's sudden reservations notwithstanding.

Meanwhile, not so very far away...

James stepped into his Upper Brook Street townhouse and handed his coat and hat to his butler, Benson.

After parting ways with Freddy at the top of the street, his thoughts had predictably returned to Miranda, where he was starting to suspect Hawthorne wasn't the real issue here.

Could he really stand aside as Miranda wed someone else—anybody else?

Disturbingly, the odd catch to his chest suggested, '*Hell no*'.

James snorted and headed toward his study.

If he were going to seriously consider such matters, he'd require no little fortification.

He only managed two steps before his butler's grim pronouncement forestalled him.

"Beg pardon, my lord, but Lady Stanton and Miss Cecily await you in the drawing room."

"Good God, Benson," James said, spinning back around. "Why the devil didn't you say at once? I'd have marched straight back outside again."

"Indeed, my lord," Benson intoned with an impassive look.

James blew out his breath.

Not his butler's fault, the dragon lady having arrived unannounced.

There was nothing for it but to get the painful interview over with.

"Organize a tray, Benson. Nothing too elaborate, though. We wouldn't want our guests getting too comfortable."

"Already taken care of, my lord."

"Good, good." James dismissed the ever-efficient butler with a wave.

With any luck, his guests would've already taken their fill and were well on their way to departure.

When he entered the parlor, however, the first thing he noticed was his stepmother's untouched plate. But then, the old harpy probably lived off her spite alone, thus didn't require the sustenance.

"Stepmother, Cecily, good day. To what do I owe the unexpected pleasure?"

Cecily offered him a shy smile while his stepmother only scowled. "It's fine time you graced us with your presence, James," Muriel returned by way of greeting.

Swallowing a retort, James took a seat. "I apologize for the delay, madam. Of course, if you'd advised me of your intention to call, I would have adjusted my schedule accordingly."

By accordingly, he would've ensured to be far from home.

Muriel's lips pinched. "As if I need to schedule a time to see my dearest stepson."

Since he was her only stepson, James took the endearment with a healthy measure of salt. Besides, the termagant hardly made a habit of popping by, *praise God*.

He narrowed his eyes at the sudden suspicion. "Has something untoward happened to prompt this visit? One of my stepsisters in trouble, mayhap?"

He slid a glance to Cecily, but she was too focused on the tightly clasped hands in her lap to offer much insight.

He looked back to his stepmother as she sputtered. "Of course not! You'd be hard pressed to find two finer ladies. Your sisters are the epitome of propriety."

James raised his brows.

Whilst perhaps true in Cecily's case, the same could hardly be said of the eldest, Jane, who'd married that marquis of hers under rather havey-cavey circumstances. Not that the whispers had bothered James overmuch. He'd been simply relieved to have one of his stepsisters off his hands.

"In fact," Muriel continued sternly, "we are here out of concern for you."

James couldn't have acted more surprised if he tread the boards on a nightly basis. "Me? What, pray tell, could've possibly warranted such concern over me?"

Muriel took on an incredulous look. "Naturally, it's all over Town, James. Your decision to finally settle down and secure the earldom is admirable to be sure. Long overdue some might even venture. But to have set your sights on Miranda Drayton of all people. Why, the idea's preposterous!" She waved a hand at him. "Well? What have you to say for yourself?"

Nothing good, that was for certain. But he only aired coldly, "Is that so, madam? Oddly enough, I cannot recall relaying any such intention to you, or indeed to anyone. And even if it is as you say—which I am by no means affirming—I cannot see how it could concern you."

Muriel snorted. "As if it is necessary to *tell* anyone, my dear boy. You made your intentions clear from the onset, singling out Miss Drayton from the moment you stepped into the Cumberland's ballroom. And of course, it concerns me. I hold you as close to my heart as I do my own flesh and blood."

James doubted the woman even possessed said organ. "Whilst I appreciate the motherly concern, Muriel, such conjecture is absurd. Why should anyone be surprised if I conversed with Miss Drayton or danced with her even? Everyone knows of the familial connection."

Muriel wasn't moved by his argument, however. "I'm no simpleton, James. The way your eyes followed the chit's every move said it all. I was not the only one to notice either, mark my words. Why you're even bothering with the upstart truly confounds me. It's common knowledge Sir Richard intends her for Lord Hawthorne, so you've barely a look in. Besides, you could have any belle of the ball, and I can name a dozen at least, more worthy of the Stanton name." She shook her head. "No. I will not stand by and let you tarnish our esteemed name with one such as she!"

'*Let me tarnish*,' indeed.

Was it any wonder James had escaped to Rose Manor as often as he had, when this was what he had to contend with at home?

Bad enough his stepmother insulting him, but he wasn't about to let her malign Miranda in his very own parlor. Whatever his intentions may or may not be.

"Miss Drayton has integrity, for one. She's not after some fop's fortune or title," he forced out between gritted teeth.

Muriel harrumphed. "If you believe that, then you're more naïve than I even imagined. The problem is you haven't been introduced to a proper girl yet. Which is where I come in, my boy. I suggest we start with an intimate gathering at Stanton House, where I'll invite only the most gracious and deserving ladies of my vast acquaintance. Then you can take your pick."

He would rather stick several cravat pins in his eyes and twist them. Repeatedly. "Certainly not! I'm perfectly capable of finding my own countess when the time comes, thank you very much."

"Since you are making such remarkable progress so far..."

James stiffened. "I've been back in society for two days, madam. You could give a man a chance."

"That's precisely why I've come to offer my assistance!" Astoundingly, the woman could twist even the harshest criticism to her own benefit. "I've already arranged one marvelous match, so I would hardly abandon my own son to his fate. It's what the late earl would have wanted in any case."

"For Christ's sake, Muriel, leave my father out of this!"

Her look could have frozen the Pacific—twice over. "Crass language doesn't become you, James. You've been consorting with undesirables long enough and could do well with some civilizing."

Hissing out his breath, James couldn't escape the fact his manners left much to be desired. So he turned apologetically to his stepsister. "Pray forgive me my lapse, Cecily."

Cecily smiled shyly in return.

Nice to know not all his relations were completely set against him.

Returning to the Dowager Countess, he raised his hand. "All I ask is a sennight, Muriel. The chance to reacquaint myself with society before we revisit this discussion. Are we agreed?"

He would be safely installed at Rose Manor by then, and well beyond his stepmother's reach.

Muriel looked set to argue but, perhaps sensing she'd pushed him as far as he would allow for one afternoon, made her own rare concession. "Fair enough," she said, before turning to Cecily with a smug, "You see, I knew he would listen to reason!"

Groaning internally, James looked to the ceiling. Instead of divine deliverance, though, all he found was a stray cobweb.

"As much as I have found the visit enlightening, Step-mother," he said, rising from his seat. "I've much to attend to this evening. Therefore, I'm afraid I must bid you and Cecily a good day."

Whilst clearly displeased by the dismissal, Muriel could do little but follow his lead. "Come, Cecily. It appears our visit is to be cut short as your brother has errands to attend to. Ones more pertinent than *his own family*."

James had Benson show them out, then he headed to the sideboard and poured himself a generous measure of brandy. He welcomed the burn as the liquor slid down his throat.

Contrary to his stepmother's assertions, he'd come back to ensure Miranda's welfare, not to make a play for her him-self. Even if she tempted him beyond measure and caused him to question his long-held conviction not to wed any-time soon.

Oh, James knew he couldn't escape his responsibilities forever. But he was only four and twenty, and marriage was an irreversible step. After seeing how his mother's passing had decimated his father, he wasn't exactly keen to subject himself to the same fate.

Downing the rest of his brandy, James moved to the study and replenished his glass from the decanter on his desk.

He took a seat and his mind wandered back to his younger days at Stanton House. When he would sneak into his father's study, curious to see what kept his sire occupied there for hours on end. His father had always discovered him, of course, and would beckon James over to sit on his knee. There, James would spin the Terrestrial globe perched on the edge of the desk and close his eyes as he brought the great orb to a stop with his finger. His father would then weave the most fantastical tales about wherever his finger had happened to land.

Odd how he rarely thought of those happier times. The times before his mother's death, and before he lost his father to his grief. Instead, James had come to associate Stanton House with the cold bleakness that had become his childhood afterwards. *After* his mother had succumbed to her long and debilitating illness, and *after* his father's withdrawal and hasty remarriage to Muriel, which had only compounded matters further.

And the lesson he'd taken from it all? That life was much easier—indeed safer—if he kept everyone at arm's length. One wouldn't get hurt that way.

Not so long after, he'd started spending more time at Rose Manor. And with Rose Manor came Miranda.

James smiled and leaned back in his chair.

Even at six Miranda had been a force to be reckoned with, entirely impossible to ignore and inordinately easy to tease. She'd been a delightful distraction from the pains James had been desperate to escape. But more than that, she'd been his playmate, his friend. Around her, he didn't feel quite so alone.

It wasn't until she fatefully kissed him that night that James had been forced to admit he'd been fooling himself. Far from being removed, all it took was the innocent touch of her lips to his for all his carefully constructed walls to come tumbling down. Furthermore, caught in Miranda's embrace, his response had hardly been friend-like in nature. Hell, he'd come within a hair's breadth of backing her against the nearest wall and ravishing her senseless. In his godmother's hallway, where anyone could have stumbled across them, for goodness' sake!

Thankfully, reason had reared its head before he'd gotten too carried away. Still, he'd been so shaken by the encounter, he could do little but react on instinct. So he did what came naturally—what he was most practiced at—he laughed off the incident and got the heck out of there.

He'd never intended to stay away for quite so long. But with distance came clarity. Away from Miranda, he could simply dismiss his feelings as a passing fancy. A natural progression from his boyhood affection, even. Miranda had grown into an alluring woman, so was it any wonder he'd reacted as any man in his position would?

But now that she was seriously considering another, he had to face what he'd recklessly cast aside. He'd certainly never felt anything close to what he'd felt for Miranda with any other woman. And seeing her again only proved those feelings hadn't dissipated with time. If anything, they'd intensified.

James waited for the inevitable feeling of panic to surface with such a revelation. But strangely, it didn't eventuate. Did that mean he was ready to take that final leap? To admit Miranda was the only one he could truly care for? Already did, if he were being brutally honest.

One thing was certain: he wouldn't achieve much sitting here brooding over his brandy. So he put down his glass and scratched around his desk for some parchment. After locating a blank sheet, he quickly penned a note to his godmother.

By the time he and Miranda next met, he'd ensure to have a plan of action in place. And if Miranda wanted a fight, James was more than happy to oblige, for he knew who would ultimately prevail in this battle of wills.

He had the most to lose, after all.

9

The Unwanted Guest

At four the following afternoon, Miranda joined her mother, father, and Lucinda in the family carriage for the short ride to Sommerville House for Lady Sommerville's soirée. They could easily have walked, the distance a quarter mile at most. But arriving on foot would've given the wrong impression entirely.

"I don't know why we have to go," Lucinda complained, looking longingly to the window.

"You know why, daughter," the colonel retorted.

She turned to him with a pout. "Well, I don't know why *I* had to come then."

"You never know," their father mused, raising his bushy brows. "You might come across a suitor willing to overlook your impertinence. One lives in hope."

Miranda hid a smile thinking it would take a very special someone to take her sister on. Lucinda was never backward in coming forward when it came to her opinions.

"I doubt we'll see anyone of interest at all," Lucinda continued to bemoan. "Just the same old set, each sennight without fail."

A sharp look from the colonel was all it took, Lucinda retreating to her corner of the coach with a sigh.

In the ensuing silence, Miranda played with the folds of her skirt.

She knew she looked the part. She'd chosen her favorite peach gown purposely to bolster her confidence. But it had made little difference in the end. She was dreading the evening seemingly as much as her sister.

She still hadn't decided how best to approach Lord Hawthorne after yesterday's debacle. If indeed she and the viscount were even on speaking terms. But before she could consider it further, they were pulling up in front of Sommerville House.

Stepping onto the pavement, Miranda contemplated the building's white façade.

"Impressive, isn't it?" her father said. "To think, you'll be mistress of all this one day."

The appearance of Lady Sommerville's starched-up butler at the door saved Miranda from formulating a reply. Then in no time at all, she found herself in the front parlor with a concoction from their hostess' famed Penwork tea chest in hand.

Lucinda stood beside her, and they sipped their tea as they took in the opulent surrounds.

Richly decorated in emerald and gold, the room contained a mismatch of gilded chaises, wingback chairs and occasional tables, which made mingling quite the challenge. As such, the guests had made the most of the available space, dividing themselves into succinct clusters interspersed between the furnishings.

"Even Christopher's company would be preferable to this!" Lucinda declared after a cursory sweep of the room. "If I'm to expire from boredom, please inform Death I'm more than ready to go."

Miranda was all amusement, seeing they'd arrived not ten minutes hence. But in truth, she too would have appreciated Emily's and her brother's presence.

Most of the assembled guests were of their father's set, thus hardly their contemporaries.

Nevertheless, Miranda couldn't resist the opportunity to rib her sister for once. "For one always touting their dislike, you do happen to mention Kit an awful lot."

"Only because he is so vexing! I'm convinced he sets out to annoy me deliberately."

Miranda stifled a laugh. "More than likely seeing you're always quick to respond in kind, sister dearest. Much to Emily's and my continual entertainment."

Lucinda frowned. "I am pleased someone finds the situation amusing."

Catching the colonel's speaking glance from across the room, Miranda schooled her expression. "Have a care, Lu. Father is scowling our way."

Lucinda straightened automatically. "Don't you find it tedious being such the perfect daughter all the time?" she asked from the corner of her mouth.

"It's not so difficult. Mayhap you should try it sometime. Practice makes perfect, you know."

"No, thank you. I'm happy to leave that to your expertise."

Miranda shot her sister a fond glance before turning back to the assembled guests.

Lady Sommerville held pride of place in the center of the room, keeping a careful watch over the proceedings from her throne-like chair.

Meeting her gaze, Miranda said to Lucinda, "Lady Sommerville is beckoning me over, so I best join her."

"I will see to Mother then." Lucinda smirked as she headed in the opposite direction.

Since Lady Sommerville wasn't Lucinda's prospective mother-in-law, Miranda couldn't blame her sister for the deflection.

She placed down her teacup and made her way across the room.

"My lady," she said, dipping into a curtesy. "May I commend you on another successful turn out. The pianist you selected for the evening is impressive indeed."

"As well he should be," Lady Sommerville said, waving a hand to the empty chaise beside her, where Miranda promptly took a seat. "Herr Albrecht hails from Berlin and wasn't easy to secure, I can assure you."

They turned to the pianoforte as the musician launched into one of Beethoven's more vigorous movements.

Miranda could only admire his deft fingertips as they danced across the keys.

"Your mother and sister look well," Lady Sommerville said, turning to peer at Miranda's family once the pianist had quietened again. "Your sister's a little highly strung though, I would think."

"Lucinda is young yet, my lady, and will surely mature with age."

"Hmm." Lady Sommerville looked doubtful. "And you, my girl? How do you keep yourself suitably engaged?"

"I enjoy assisting my mother in managing Drayton House, and we support the war widows as oft we can. Then, of course, there is reading and needlepoint," Miranda said, though it felt odd listing her accomplishments on rote.

"But do you play?" Lady Sommerville looked pointedly toward the grand pianoforte where Herr Albrecht was now expertly thrumming out one of Handel's elegant sonatas.

"Tolerably well, my lady." Miranda dearly hoped she would never be expected to perform for such a crowd, though.

"I trust you're not subjecting Miss Drayton to an inquisition, Mother," Lord Hawthorne said, suddenly appearing by Miranda's right shoulder.

Miranda exhaled as she rose to greet the viscount.

Lady Sommerville's voice softened as she addressed her son. "Certainly not, dearest. Miss Drayton and I were merely becoming better acquainted."

Miranda smiled.

It was true in a manner of speaking.

"Then you won't mind if I steal the lady for a turnabout the room," Lord Hawthorne said, turning his gaze to Miranda. "If you're amenable, Miss Drayton?"

"I'd be most obliged, Lord Hawthorne, thank you."

As much as Miranda dreaded the upcoming conversation, it couldn't be any worse than a public interview with the man's mother.

"Yes, do go and enjoy yourselves." The countess waved them away before looking to her next target.

Miranda placed her hand on Lord Hawthorne's arm, and he steered her through the crowd to the outer edge of the room.

"Well, you appear no worse for wear after Mother's grilling."

Miranda let out a surprised chuckle. Levity was the last thing she'd expected from him. "It was hardly a grilling, Lord Hawthorne. I can handle myself in any case."

He considered her thoughtfully. "Yes, I've come to appreciate that."

Miranda's cheeks heated.

Perhaps all was not lost.

She seemed to have passed Lady Sommerville's unwritten test, and the viscount didn't look too put out after their recent exchange of words.

"Your look turned quite serious then, Miss Drayton. Nothing amiss, I hope?"

"Not at all," Miranda assured him.

She smiled as the viscount led her toward the piano. The pianist had reached his final crescendo and was taking a bow.

She joined the viscount in applause.

"What a moving performance," she said. "Music must be one of our greatest accomplishments, wouldn't you agree?"

"Music certainly has its place—" A disconcerting hush descended over the room before the viscount could finish.

Miranda turned and was stunned to see her Aunt Bethel enter the drawing room, accompanied by James of all people.

"Stanton certainly knows how to make an entrance," the viscount muttered.

James looked about the room and caught Miranda's eye. His lips twitched as if fully aware of the stir he'd created. *The irrepressible rogue.*

"Dear Lady Sommerville," the Dowager Duchess said, her voice carrying across the room. "I sincerely apologize for my tardiness. Mrs. Barlow was unfortunately indisposed at the last minute and sends her regrets. But as luck would have it, I was able to secure this fine escort in her stead." She smiled at their hostess, seemingly oblivious to the audience that was hanging on her every word.

James bowed. "A pleasure to see you again, my lady. I hope I am not intruding."

"Of course not, Lord Stanton. You are most welcome," Lady Sommerville said, dispensing any awkwardness with a flick of her wrist. "Please help yourself to the refreshments. I'm sure you are already acquainted with everyone present."

James nodded before heading toward the sideboard whilst the Dowager Duchess accepted Lady Sommerville's invitation to sit.

As there was little more to see, the guests returned to their conversations, albeit with furtive glances in James' direction.

Miranda dampened down her dismay, turning to the viscount as he remarked, "Don't you find it odd, Miss Drayton? Stanton suddenly appearing wherever you happen to be."

"A coincidence, surely." Miranda dearly hoped anyway.

"That remains to be seen, and look, he's making his way over," he said, adding a faint, "Surprise, surprise," under his breath.

Miranda drew herself up as James approached, her treacherous heart pumping madly all the while.

"Stanton, this is a surprise," the viscount said. "This must be, what, three times in as many days?"

James smiled. "Ah, Hawthorne. I'm flattered you noticed."

Miranda shot James a reproachful look.

If he was intent on making mischief, he was doing a fine job of it. The viscount was positively teeming with disdain.

"Lord Stanton," she said, "it's a shame you arrived late. You missed Herr Albrecht's performance, the talented pianist hailing all the way from Berlin."

James momentarily abandoned his childish standoff with Lord Hawthorne to respond. "That is a pity, Miss Drayton. For knowing your love of music as I surely do, he must be a true maestro to have earned such esteem."

Miranda frowned.

She didn't appreciate how familiar James sounded as it hardly went any way to diffusing the situation.

James' gaze brightened. "And may I add, you look well this evening. Peach becomes you admirably."

Hearing the hiss of Lord Hawthorne's breath, Miranda laid a hand on his sleeve.

To James, she said sweetly, "You are too kind, my lord," whilst shooting him imaginary daggers with her eyes. Then inspiration struck. She swept a hand toward the colonel. "Oh look, there's my father. He was only saying how he regretted missing you at the Cumberland rout and is keen to renew your acquaintance."

As it so happened, her father was looking in their direction, although his expression tilted more toward brooding than welcoming.

James flashed an ironic smile. "I will head straight over then, shall I? One would so hate to disappoint. Until later, Miss Drayton. Viscount."

"Stanton." Lord Hawthorne all but snarled as he watched James' retreat, not speaking again until the earl was safely situated on the opposing side of the room.

"What is between you and Stanton," he said. "And I insist on an answer this time."

Miranda closed her eyes, using the moment to gather her wits. Although she knew she couldn't avoid the question forever.

She looked back to Lord Hawthorne. "Honestly, there's nothing between us at all. Before Lady Cumberland's ball, I hadn't set eyes on Lord Stanton for years, and his presence this evening is just a surprise to me as it is to you."

Considering it was the absolute truth, the viscount could hardly find fault with her words.

Lord Hawthorne didn't seem satisfied by her explanation, however. "Be that as it may, Miss Drayton, I feel I must bid you caution. I don't trust the bounder at all, and I find his sudden return to society rather suspect. Inconveniently coincidental, I would even venture."

Miranda had the mad urge to laugh. For hadn't she only been thinking the very same thing? Not that she would readily admit it, especially within the viscount's earshot.

"You've need not concern yourself, my lord. I'm not so easily turned by smooth talk and a pretty head."

"I did not mean to imply that you would," he returned. "Your common sense is as infallible as it is admirable. Enough talk of Stanton. I for one refuse to let him ruin our evening."

Miranda nodded, thinking it the most sensible notion she'd heard all afternoon.

James' gut clenched to hear the colonel's depiction of the conditions his men had endured, and by all accounts were still enduring, on the Continent.

"I agree, enough is enough, and it's been allowed to continue long enough," James said. "As such, I'll ensure to be at Lords for the presentation of your bill, Sir Richard."

"Capital! I knew you were a reasonable fellow and I could count on your support," the colonel said, with what James suspected was a smile lurking beneath his bushy whiskers.

James was similarly pleased, because in Miranda's attempt to get rid of him, she had granted him an unexpected boon. The opportunity to present himself to her father as a worthy contender for her hand.

His gaze drifted to Miranda and his stomach tightened for another reason altogether.

She was laughing at something Hawthorne had said.

"What are your intentions, Stanton?"

James turned back to eye Miranda's father steadily.

Was he truly about to cast his hat into the ring?

"They are entirely honorable, sir, I assure you," he heard himself say.

Sounded like he just did.

Apart from a slight twitch to his right cheek, Sir Richard's expression didn't waver. "Understood. However, I feel it's only fair to warn, you're rather late to the front, thus face an uphill battle."

James wasn't the least surprised by the pronouncement. The colonel would hardly sacrifice Hawthorne that readily. But being underestimated only strengthened his resolve.

"Don't they say something's not important unless it's worth fighting for, or something to that effect?"

The colonel took a moment to weigh his measure. "True enough. I'll wish you the best of luck then, Stanton, shall I?"

Whilst James could appreciate the colonel's irony, he suspected 'luck' wouldn't quite cover it. Especially if Miranda kept avoiding him, this 'wooing by room-length' hardly furthering his cause.

As the colonel moved away, James looked for an opening to approach Miranda, but she remained attached to Hawthorne's side all evening. Instead, he found an unexpected ally in her sister.

"Lord Stanton." Lucinda called from her position by the refreshment table. "How pleased I am to see you. You certainly liven up what would otherwise be a dull evening indeed."

"Miss Lucinda." James came to stand beside her and passed her a plate. "You're not enjoying the soirée then, I take it."

"I'm liking it much better *now*," she said, spearing three slices of roast beef and sliding them onto her dish. "I fear you must be the most interesting person here, bar myself of course."

James chuckled. "Considering you find the company so lacking, then why attend at all?"

"As if I was offered the choice. But thankfully these evenings don't drag on too long since everyone has somewhere to be afterwards."

"Oh," James said, pretending to consider what little remained of the buffet. "And do you have another engagement this evening?"

Lucinda grinned as she swiped the last meat pie from beneath his nose. "Not tonight, but tomorrow's another story. We never miss Lady Fairbottom's annual musicale, and I have an inkling we might see you there."

James returned her smile. "It's odd how these things turn out, don't you think?"

10

A Reluctant Observer

The following evening, Miranda was seated by Lord Hawthorne amongst the other hundred or so guests that lined Lady Fairbottom's ballroom. The annual concert was mostly a family affair, providing a convenient platform within which the countess' daughters could display their accomplishments.

Unfortunately for the second daughter, Lady Samantha, the musical talent seemed to have skipped over her when it had passed down the family. And she was acutely aware of it too, wincing as she hit F instead of F sharp in her pianoforte recital. But despite her fumbles, the audience applauded her performance just as enthusiastically as they had her elder sister, Lady Violet, before her.

"Good show," Lord Hawthorne commended from his seat beside Miranda. "Handel is a fitting choice at these gatherings. Wouldn't you agree?"

Miranda concurred, for it would be almost sacrilegious not to.

Hush resettled over the crowd as the youngest daughter, Lady Mabel, took to the stage. At barely five and ten, the budding violinist scanned the crowd with a confidence that belittled her years.

Miranda leaned forward in her seat, eager to hear what piece Lady Mabel would gift them. She wasn't disappointed, the young lady executing Mozart's Violin Concerto No. 5 with deceptive ease. What Miranda would give for even a tenth of her talent.

With the concert concluded, Miranda sighed contentedly.

"You appear fatigued, my lady," Lord Hawthorne said. "Come, let us go in search of some refreshment."

Not bothering to correct his misapprehension, Miranda stood and took his proffered arm. "I'd never say no to a pastry or two."

At the buffet table, Miranda selected a particularly juicy-looking lobster tartlet and popped it into her mouth.

Lord Hawthorne's attention wasn't on their hostess' impressive spread, however. "Looks like our friend has decided to grace society with his presence yet again this evening."

Miranda carefully swallowed before responding. "So it would seem."

No need to speculate which gentleman the viscount so referred.

She could hardly have missed James' arrival, with him being late to take his seat beside Aunt Bethel and Meg, two rows to the front of where Miranda sat with the viscount. Indeed, James had remained irritatingly in her peripheral throughout the recital, even though she'd made a concerted effort to keep her focus upon the stage. And she thought she'd made a fair showing of ignorance. That was until the viscount had the temerity to bring him up.

"His motive this time, I wonder." Lord Hawthorne scowled. "It's not as if he can offer up Mrs. Barlow as an excuse seeing she looks remarkably restored from whatever ailed her just yesterday."

In fact, Meg seemed vastly entertained by whatever tale James was currently spinning.

Miranda was unable to shake the sneaking suspicion that Lord Hawthorne might have the right of it. James turning up like the proverbial bad penny couldn't be purely by chance. His motive, though, was anyone's guess.

She'd given up trying to understand the fellow eons ago.

As if sensing her regard, James' gaze shifted her way, and she quickly turned her head aside. "Whatever Lord Stanton's reasoning, it need not concern us."

Lord Hawthorne nodded. "Would you care for a stroll on the terrace? It looks most pleasant out."

Since James had made a move toward her mother and Lucinda, Miranda couldn't agree to the suggestion quickly enough.

Stepping onto the balcony, they were embraced by a summery breeze. They sidestepped a group of guests who were traversing the length of the terrace and came to rest in a sheltered corner.

Stopping by the balustrade, Lord Hawthorne looked to the darkened garden beyond. "Regrettably, I'm unable to call on you tomorrow as I'm to accompany my father to the House of Lords."

"Pray do not concern yourself on my account, Lord Hawthorne. My father's bill is being tabled, is it not?"

"Indeed, it is," the viscount confirmed without venturing anything further.

Curious, Miranda asked his opinion on how her father's proposal was likely to be received.

"The colonel will face some stiff opposition, I'm afraid," he said. "Many are of the mind the monies necessary to fund such an endeavor would be better served strengthening our battlements on the field."

As his tone suggested he was one of that number, she felt compelled to point out, "That's short-sighted, surely. If our men keep dying because of the lack of supplies my father is calling to light, there will be no regiment left to fight, then where would our campaign be?"

Not to mention the unnecessary human cost.

He shrugged. "There's no concern of that. Not when there are plenty awaiting in the ridges, ready to replenish the troops as and when needed."

Miranda wasn't the least comforted by the assertion. As if one soldier could easily be replaced with another! Her stomach rolled, thinking of the colonel's intention to buy Jonathan a commission as soon as he came of age.

"But every soldier is someone's father, uncle, or brother..." she said, her voice catching on the last.

"Evidently, but a man can't be blind to the risks he faces upon enlisting," he declared, leaving Miranda dumbfounded by his cavalier attitude.

And what of her father? If all his hard work amounted to naught, he would be devastated. She could only hope the viscount had overestimated the expected resistance to his proposal.

Lord Hawthorne spoke of other things then, the soldiers' plight seemingly forgotten.

How easy it was to dismiss an issue when it didn't affect one directly.

James had the odd sensation he'd been in this exact situation before, unable to do little but watch as Hawthorne stole Miranda away to the Fairbottom's terrace. He sincerely hoped it wasn't a precursor of the future.

Thinking himself clever, he'd sought out Miranda's family post-performance, knowing she'd have to return to their side eventually. Then he could have spoken with her at least.

But Hawthorne had blindsided him once again.

James supposed he should give the man credit where credit was due, but all he felt was a compulsion to bloody someone. Preferably a certain someone with a sardonic set of gray eyes and an ingrained disposition toward pomposity.

However, violence never solved anything. At least, that's what his dear mother used to say.

So James didn't storm the terrace as sorely tempted. Instead, he turned back to Lady Nora and Lucinda and picked up the conversation where he'd left off.

"Whatever happened next, Lord Stanton?" Lucinda asked, her eyes watering in her effort to contain her giggles. "When your Latin tutor discovered his implements had been inexplicably fixed to his desk?"

James smiled as he recalled the incident, just one of the many scrapes he and Freddy had gotten themselves into at Eton. "Mr. Masters was justifiably incensed and, as no one dared point the finger at us, he made the entire class memorize *The Distichs of Cato* as punishment and recite them *verbatim* at assembly the following morning."

"You and Lord Camden would have been popular after that, I expect."

The minx seemed to delight at the prospect.

"That's one way of putting it," he said. "Several lads took particular exception to the punishment, ambushing Freddy and me in our beds later that night."

They'd been battered and sore for a sennight in fact. But Freddy had agreed the bruises had been worth it, to see Mr. Masters' face...

As Lucinda gave her giggles free rein, James recalled Miranda's reaction when he'd shared the same tale with her not so long after the incident. Far from being amused, she'd scolded him for acting so juvenile.

James smiled at the memory.

Shocking Miranda had been one of his favorite pastimes. Now, he'd give anything just to hear her laugh.

With that sobering thought, he focused back on his companions and found Lady Nora had gone deathly pale.

"Miranda's been gone quite some time," she said, clutching onto Lucinda's arm. "You may need to find her, Lucinda dear, for I fear one of my megrims is taking hold."

"Don't fret, Mama," Lucinda reassured her. "I will fetch her right away."

"Please, allow me," James interjected.

It was the least he could do considering he'd failed to notice her mother's distress.

"Thank you, James. If it is not too much of an inconvenience," Lady Nora said.

"Pray don't concern yourself, my lady. I am more than happy to assist."

He couldn't have Lady Nora thinking herself a nuisance.

She rallied a smile. "You've always been a lovely boy."

Swallowing his surprise at the unexpected declaration, James made for the terrace, directing a passing footman to summon the Drayton carriage whilst he was at it.

Stepping into the balmy night, he scanned the shadows and quickly placed Hawthorne cozening up to Miranda by the balustrade.

"Miss Drayton," he called out, striding toward them.

Miranda and Hawthorne moved apart as if they'd been caught doing something untoward.

"Stanton," Hawthorne said.

James barely acknowledged him.

"Your mother has taken ill and needs to return home," he said to Miranda, wishing he had more time to appreciate how stunning she looked bathed in the soft moonlight.

Miranda looked to Hawthorne, concern furrowing her brow. "I must go to her at once."

Hawthorne took her arm. "Of course, my dear. I'll take you to her." He then drew Miranda away, shooting James a smug look from over his shoulder. *The arse.*

James curled his hand into a fist.

So much for sweeping in and saving the day. Or evening. Saving much of anything, in fact.

He couldn't recall a time when he felt more redundant.

Watching Miranda glide away on Hawthorne's arm seemed the worst kind of punishment. Even when Miranda paused by the door to mouth him a silent 'thank you' didn't mollify him much.

Surely, his life wouldn't be forever confined to these snippets of Miranda's time only to have her snatched away again. It was all too depressing to contemplate.

At this rate, he would never get Miranda in one place long enough to converse, let alone convince her of the possibility of a *them*.

Obviously, Hawthorne had to be removed from the scene post-haste. For some inexplicable reason Miranda seemed to like the fellow, although personally, James couldn't fathom the attraction.

Separating the pair was the only way forward, and he knew just the place to push his advantage.

He strode back into the Fairbottom's ballroom with renewed purpose.

Miranda best be prepared, for he was coming for her.

11

Secrets and Half-Truths

Miranda and Lucinda were quiet on the carriage ride home in respect for their mother, who only turned greener with every dip and sway of the carriage.

Miranda just hoped it wasn't a bad attack which would keep her abed for days.

Their mother's megrims were debilitating as they were unpredictable, and they only seemed to increase in frequency as the season progressed.

Seeing the toll the season took on her mother, Miranda couldn't help but feel guilty. The quicker she wed, the quicker she could take over the chaperoning of her sisters so her mother could retire from society in peace.

The colonel, unsurprisingly, had elected to remain at the Fairbottom's in a last bid attempt to rack up support for his bill. Shame the concern he showed for his men had never extended to his wife.

Miranda was grateful that Lord Hawthorne promised to be a more considerate husband.

Begrudgingly, she had to admit that James had surprised her as well. Whilst looking none too pleased when he first stepped onto the terrace, she didn't doubt his genuine concern for her mother. She should have thanked him properly before rushing off.

Lady Nora moaned, drawing back her attention.

Her priority was to get her mother settled. Then she would find a way through the quagmire she'd somehow gotten herself into.

***

An hour later, Lady Nora was comfortably tucked up in her bed with a lavender compress at her brow and a draft of chamomile tea by her bedside. After softly bidding their good nights, Miranda and Lucinda slipped from the room.

They headed downstairs to the library by silent accord, where Lucinda immediately took the colonel's favorite chair by the fireside. "Personally, I'm not disappointed that our evening was precipitously brought to an end," she said.

Having settled onto the adjacent sofa, Miranda looked over in surprise. "Why, whatever happened? The last I saw of it, you and Mother were hanging onto James every word. Did the earl say something to upset you?"

Lucinda laughed and shot back to her feet. "Heavens, no. James was nothing but entertaining. There are certain gentlemen—and I use that term loosely—who embody the exact opposite, however. But we'll need a nightcap if we're to discuss the supposed merits of the opposing sex."

Contrary to her words, she bypassed liquor cabinet and headed to the bookshelves lining the back wall.

Seeing her pause by their father's extensive collection of political discourses, Miranda had to ask, "You haven't caught Mother's malady by any chance?"

"One would think so." Lucinda frowned as she dug around the bookcase. She made a triumphant sound then turned back with a grin, prize in hand.

"How on earth...?" Miranda started to ask before falling silent.

She didn't really want to know how her sister knew of the bottle of port hidden within the library shelves.

Lucinda removed the stopper and took a healthy swig.

Miranda coughed. "Would it have been too much to use a glass?"

"And leave the evidence lying around? You might grant me more foresight than that," Lucinda quipped, crossing back to the fireplace, and extending the bottle to Miranda as she took back her seat.

Miranda eyed the offering. "But won't Father be suspicious to find his wine has mysteriously disappeared overnight?"

"Perhaps. But he can hardly accuse anyone of theft without first admitting to the stash now, can he?" She wriggled the bottle. "Come on, Mira, you know Father only hides the best vintages."

Miranda accepted the port without further argument and took a tentative sip. The wine had a pleasant fruity taste and slid easily past the tongue. No wonder her father took such pains to conceal the stuff.

She handed the bottle back to Lucinda and settled into the cushions. She would need her faculties intact if she were to have any hope of figuring out her next step.

Lucinda shot her a contemplative look. "Why so glum, chum? I know we had an unfortunate end to the evening, but instinct tells me something else is going on with you."

Miranda smiled.

Those who disregarded Lucinda's instincts did so at their peril.

"I must marry, that's all. The sooner the better."

Lucinda paused, bottle halfway to her lips. "Well, *that's* a given, but why the sudden urgency? You haven't found yourself in a compromising position, have you?"

"Of course not!"

Lucinda looked disappointed. "Didn't think so. Lord Hawthorne hardly seems the type."

"You say that like it's a bad thing." Miranda took back the bottle and chuckled. "Still, I worry over my lack of progress. I'm not getting any younger, and once I'm settled, it would clear the way for you—"

Lucinda cut her off with a laugh. "Don't hasten on my account, Mira. Goodness, could you imagine it?" She reclined in the chair and draped the back of her hand across her brow. "Oh, my fair prince, you do me the greatest honor. Of course, I'd be delighted to be crowned your princess. But alas, we must hold off until my elder sister is wed, even if I'm marked for the grave by the time she gets within a foot of an altar."

Miranda eyed her ironically. "Fair enough, I concede your point. It's only that these past two years I've been trapped in a limbo of sorts, somewhere between assumed but not officially engaged. A state that can hardly go on forever."

Lucinda nodded, all knowing. "It's easy to see how you would become so comfortable."

Miranda frowned. "Comfortable? In what sense?"

"Well, mid-way through your first season, Father decided only the viscount would do, and as you didn't question his choice, society deemed you settled. From then on you needed only wait to have your future handed to you, trussed up all nice and proper."

Miranda leaned forward. Could it really be that simple?

But no. She hadn't just 'gone along' with the colonel because it was the easiest option. She'd also come to the same decision herself.

"It needn't be that way, though!" Lucinda suddenly exclaimed, shooting to her feet and pacing the length of the rug. "Whatever happened, Mira?" She stopped to ask. "When we were younger, you longed for your own knight in shining armor almost as much as I did."

Miranda straitened. "I pulled my head out of those fairytales you espouse so much and grew up!"

"If this is what growing up entails," Lucinda said, sweeping a hand over Miranda's form, "then I want no part of it.

You deserve a love match just as much as the next person, perhaps even more so."

"Who's to say I haven't found that with Lord Hawthorne, hmm?"

"Poppycock!" Lucinda crossed her arms. "You love the viscount as much as I love...state dinners with only stale political discourse on the menu!"

Miranda had to laugh, although her amusement soon died when Lucinda added, "I know all this has something to do with James."

"What could possibly make you think that?"

Lucinda rolled her eyes. "Come now, Mira. This has only come to a head since the good earl returned, and you've been acting most strangely ever since. Do you deny it?"

She certainly could try. "James has absolutely no bearing on this!"

Lucinda snorted. "Believe what you will. But then, James coming back can only be a good thing."

"However so?"

"Whatever James means to you—or doesn't, as the case may be—his return has forced you to reconsider things and decide once and for all what it is you truly want. What you want, Miranda. Not Father, nor Mother, nor the word according to society. But *you*."

Miranda huffed. "But I already know."

"Do you really?" Lucinda tutted, shaking her head. "One never forgets their first love, you do realize."

Miranda shot to her feet. "Don't be absurd, Lucinda. James never was, nor ever could be, my love!"

Besides, what did her sister know of love, apart from what she read in her storybooks? Fantastical tales that had no bearing on real life whatsoever.

"Fine, have it your way!" Lucinda tossed her head. "Let it not be said that I didn't try talking some sense into you."

"More like lecturing, sister dear," Miranda muttered. She reached to where Lucinda had placed the stopper and re-corked the bottle. She then crossed the room, returning the port to its hiding place.

The liquor had loosened their tongues quite enough for one evening.

Once she'd rearranged the books into position, she turned back to her sister. "It is what it is, Lu, and I am too weary to argue the point."

"Agreed," Lucinda said, stifling her own yawn. "If you won't listen to reason, then I can't do much about it, can I? Anyway, we best get ourselves to bed before Father returns home. We wouldn't want the dear colonel catching us mid-act, would we?"

Miranda gave a mock shiver. "Indeed, we would not."

"No need to frown, Mira," Lucinda said on their way to the stairs. "I know you will make the right decision *eventually*."

Miranda made a non-committal sound.

She'd already said all there was to say on the matter.

12

The Sour and the Sweet

The following afternoon, Miranda and Lucinda took themselves to their favorite bookstore, leaving their mother to her rest.

Stepping through the threshold, Miranda breathed in the comforting smells of leather and parchment.

Beresford's shelves were teeming with works on every subject imaginable. From the great French philosophers and the latest in medical advancements, to the vast array of novels to which Lucinda was making a beeline.

After greeting the proprietor, Miranda headed for the poetry section where a copy of Johnson's The Vanity of Human Wishes caught her eye. Picking up the slim volume, she'd just reached the stanza about stubborn choices when the tinkle of the doorbell caused her to glance up.

"I am convinced I saw her enter, Cecily!" Lady Stanton's unmistakable silhouette all but shrilled from the doorway.

"I'm sure you are correct," Lady Cecily said, hastening into the store behind her mother.

Miranda's fingers tightened around the book.

What could James' stepmother possibly want with her?

Mr. Beresford bustled over to greet the newcomers. "My dear ladies, welcome. How may I serve you this fine day?"

"Your assistance is not required, sir." Lady Stanton dismissed the bespeckled man with a flick to her wrist then proceeded toward Miranda.

Miranda carefully reshelved the volume before turning. "Lady Stanton and Lady Cecily, good day."

The Dowager Countess didn't even attempt to mask her sneer. "Do spare us the faux pleasantries if you would, Miss Drayton, for I am aware of your game."

Miranda was completely taken aback.

How was one to respond to the like?

Lucinda appeared to stand by Miranda's side, drawing Lady Stanton's imperial gaze. "I assume this to be one of your sisters," she remarked.

Lucinda hadn't been formally introduced to James' stepmother, nor did she appear keen to correct the oversight.

Miranda performed the honors in any event. "May I present my younger sister, Miss Lucinda Drayton. Lucinda, the Lady Stanton, and her youngest daughter, Lady Cecily."

Lucinda's curtsy was insultingly brief, but the Dowager Countess was too caught up in her own incivility to notice.

She gave a curt nod before turning back to Miranda. "My stepson is fully aware of his responsibilities and will choose a bride equal to his rank and station. I will not have someone of your ilk...*confusing*...him!"

Miranda stiffened at the slight but made a concerted effort to remain calm. "You need not be concerned on that account, my lady. I have no such designs on your stepson, I can assure you."

Far from being appeased, Lady Stanton's expression only tightened. "A likely tale! You may have the ton fooled with your carefully contrived innocence, missy, however I am wise to your wiles. Be forewarned, though. Such an ambition is futile and will only cause you grief. As if I would allow such a match! And if you persist on this course, I won't hesitate. I'll crush you and your sisters' reputations with but a word, then where will you all be?"

"No place good, I imagine." Miranda took in a steadying breath. She was determined to be polite to the end even if it killed her. "Such a step is unnecessary, however. I'm no one of import, especially when it comes to your stepson, thus hardly warrant the fuss."

"You will certainly find no arguments from this quarter," the Dowager Countess was quick to concur, "and so you should be aware of your place. Like attracts like after all. But do have a care, Miss Drayton, for I'll be watching most diligently."

She made sure to include Lucinda in her contemptuous look.

"Come, Cecily. I believe we are done here." The Dowager Countess swept out the door, leaving the bewildered-looking Lady Cecily little choice but to hasten after her.

Miranda could only feel sorry for the girl.

One could hardly help their relations.

Lucinda exhaled as the door closed on the pair. "Talk about dreadful! No wonder James avoids Stanton House like the plague. I would too with that shrew in residence."

Still reeling from Lady Stanton's accusations, Miranda's gaze hadn't shifted from the door.

"Are you well, Mira love?" Lucinda asked.

Miranda nodded and looked to Mr. Beresford.

The bookseller was studying his ledger most attentively and she could only hope for his continued discretion.

How dare Lady Stanton paint her as a jezebel, quick to shift her favors at the first sight of richer pickings! Everyone knew she was intended for the viscount.

Miranda could only hope that if she ignored the countess' spite, the ridiculous speculation would die a natural death.

Lucinda, on the other hand, was far less circumspect.

"How dare that woman suggest you aren't good enough for our James? Are we not of a respectable family with respectable enough portions? We certainly aren't harboring any scandalous secrets in our armoires. Our aunt married a duke for goodness' sake!"

What Lucinda said was true, still they couldn't escape the fact. Whilst their father had been born into the landed gentry and was well decorated for his military successes in Spain and Portugal, his social standing had only risen following his knighthood the previous season. Obviously, though, some were of the opinion a title didn't count unless it was passed down from birth.

"It's of no consequence, Lu," Miranda said firmly. "We know our own worth, so what's one person's misguided opinions? Besides, it's not as if I am dangling after James' hand, so I suggest we dismiss the encounter from our minds."

Lucinda shuddered. "If only it were that simple."

"What we need is a distraction. Why don't we head over to Gunter's as planned? I've lost my appetite for books, having had quite enough drama for one day."

Lucinda quickly acquiesced, so they bid the proprietor adieu and took to the street where their carriage stood wait. Climbing aboard, Miranda directed the coachman to Gunter's Tea Shop.

"Why have we stopped here?" Lucinda asked when the carriage rattled to a stop not so long afterward.

Miranda peered out the window. "I'm not sure."

The carriage door opened to reveal their head groom, Sampson.

"I'm afraid you'll have to walk from here, Miss," he said, eyeing the mismatch of coaches that covered Berkeley Square.

After handing Miranda down from the carriage, he turned to assist Lucinda.

Sighting the distance to Gunter's storefront, Lucinda groaned.

"Chin up," Miranda said. "Think of the appetite we'll amass on the walk over. Then we can order the largest serving without feeling the least guilty."

"That's assuming we make it that far. Luncheon was hours ago! If I knew I had such a trek ahead of me, I'd have pocketed a bun or two for the ride over," Lucinda groused.

Miranda grinned, feeling considerably lighter already.

Lady Stanton's accusations couldn't touch her out here in the sunshine.

She looped her hand through Lucinda's arm. "Then we best make a start before you start swooning. I doubt I could carry you the distance, and it would be a shame to miss out."

They entered the store some minutes later and were pleased to find their friend Emily seated by the front window.

"What luck!" she said, beckoning them over. "Do join us. With Father and Kit holed up in chambers all day, Amy and I decided to treat ourselves to an ice. Shame the better part of Town had the same idea," she added wryly. "Ah, here's Amy with the day's menu."

Miranda and Lucinda turned to greet Miss Primrose, Emily's old-governess-come-companion, then took the chairs across from their friends.

"What's the specialty of the day?" Lucinda asked, peering over Miranda's shoulder at the list Amy had handed her. "I'm of a mind to be daring and want to try something new."

"I'm not sure whether being adventurous at Gunter's is wise," Emily said. "I ordered the *Fromage de Parmesan* only the last week and, whilst impressively shaped into a wedge of cheese, its taste reminded me of musty old stockings."

Lucinda scrunched her nose. "Not the cheese, then. I think I'll have the pineapple and coconut instead. The combination sounds terribly exotic."

After relaying their selections to the hovering attendant—where fruit ended up being the flavor of the day—the conversation turned to the previous night's musicale.

"Wasn't Lady Mabel's performance divine?" Emily said to Miranda. "I went to speak with you afterward, but it was like you'd vanished into thin air."

"Mother developed one of her megrims, so we returned home early," Miranda explained.

Lucinda leaned forward. "Speaking of headaches, you'll never guess who stormed into Beresford's Bookstore this afternoon. Lord Stanton's ogre of a stepmother, if you can at all credit it!"

"Do keep your voice down, Lucinda," Miranda said. "We hardly want the whole of Mayfair knowing our business."

Lucinda snorted. "As if Lady Stanton gave a fig about discretion when she proceeded to tear strips off you."

Their friends looked startled.

"Whatever could you have done to earn Lady Stanton's ire, Miranda?" Emily asked. "By all accounts, you hardly know the woman."

Lucinda smiled. "She thinks our Mira has set her cap at her stepson."

Emily raised her brows. "Does she indeed? I wonder what gave her that impression."

"Heaven knows," Miranda quickly put in before her sister could start theorizing.

Their conversation was cut short by the arrival of their ices. Mayhap the only thing to go Miranda's way all day.

Turning her attention to her dish, Miranda marveled at the five perfect-looking strawberries Gunter had fashioned, which tasted as luscious as they appeared. She'd just gone back for a second spoonful when she was rudely interrupted by the voice of the last person she wished to hear.

"Good afternoon, ladies."

Miranda reluctantly raised her gaze to where James stood before them, looking all too resplendent in a bottle-green riding coat buttoned over fawn pantaloons.

Really, he couldn't look more appealing if he tried.

"Lord Stanton, what a coincidence," Lucinda exclaimed. "We were only—oof!"

Miranda silenced her with a well-aimed kick from beneath the table. "We were only saying Gunter has truly excelled himself. You're in for an absolute treat, my lord. Although, considering the crowd, you may wish to order your ice before all the best flavors are taken."

Of course, by addressing James directly, Miranda now had to weather his gaze. Never an easy task. Yet she considered it the lesser of two evils.

The less said about her altercation with his stepmother the better.

"Is that so, Miss Drayton," James said in what was little more than a rumble, which had Miranda's fingers tightening around her bowl. "Then you must tell me which flavor you chose. I shall order the same, thereby avoiding disappointment."

Miranda licked her lips in the vain hope it would spark her memory.

She could barely recall her own name let alone remember what she'd just eaten.

James tracked the movement with his eyes, and all remaining cognizant thought flew out the window.

Fortunately, Lucinda called upon herself to answer. "Oh, Mira had the strawberry as usual."

"Talk about coincidence," James said, his gaze never straying from Miranda's mouth. "Strawberry happens to be my choice favorite as well."

Miranda set her bowl on the table with a clunk.

The last of her ice had melted to slush anyway. In direct correlation with the rising temperate of the room most probably.

She stood only to step back, the action bringing her closer to James than was prudent. "We should return home to our mother. Thank you for sharing your ices with us, Emily, Miss Primrose."

Lucinda had also taken to her feet. "Yes, we enjoyed our little *vis-à-vis*," she said to their friends. "Now Miranda and I are suitably reinvigorated, we can start the hike back to our carriage—"

"Let me escort you," James offered.

"That's not necessary," Miranda put in hastily. "We wouldn't want to keep you from your treat, especially after coming all this way."

"Westminster's no great distance," he countered. "Besides, I seem to have lost my appetite—for ices, that is." He extended his arm toward her. "Shall we?"

Miranda stared at his sleeve as if it were a foreign object she wasn't at all sure what to do with.

"Miss Drayton?" he prompted.

Reaching out, she stopped shy of touching him.

James took her hand and gently placed it in the crook of his arm. "There. Much better," he said softly before turning back to the others. "Miss Burton, Miss Primrose. It's been an absolute pleasure. I trust we will meet again soon."

Miranda blinked.

Lord knew what Emily and Amy were making of the exchange.

Lucinda moved to James' other side and took his free arm. "Lead on, gallant sir."

James smiled as he led them to the front of the store, where one of Gunter's attendants held open the door.

13

New Beginnings

James steered Miranda and her sister into Berkeley Square, listening to Lucinda's natter with only half an ear.

It was difficult to concentrate with Miranda so close—so close that her lilac gown brushed his trouser leg with each and every step as they weaved their way through the assembled carriages.

With considerable effort James shifted his attention to where they were heading, then looked to Miranda with raised brows.

She waved to the general vicinity of her conveyance, so he turned in that direction.

They hadn't gone far when Lucinda pulled back. "There's Miss Browning! I *must* compliment her on her new bonnet as it's ever so flattering. Do go ahead." She waved them on. "I'll catch you up presently."

Hearing Miranda's sigh, James suppressed a smile.

Lucinda's ploy to leave them alone couldn't be plainer.

Not that he was complaining since he'd come to Gunter's in search of Miranda—her sister having let the planned outing slip the previous evening.

They left Lucinda with her friend and pressed onward.

"How is your mother?" he asked. "Much improved from last evening, I trust."

"She's resting, thank you," Miranda returned without so much as a break in stride. "The quiet will do her the world of good, and she's sure to be back to her usual self within no time."

"In time for your aunt's house party, I expect," he commented.

Miranda faltered, and he tightened his hold of her arm to steady her. But she shook him off and strode away. He hastened to keep up.

"You must be keen to repair to Hampshire as you always seemed happy there."

She stopped and turned back around. "Yes, I am. I would never pass an opportunity to visit my aunt, that hasn't changed. Although I doubt you would understand the inclination."

James raised his hands, though he was more than ready to air all their grievances.

That way, they could finally resolve matters and move on to greater things.

But before he could respond, Miranda went on to say, "It may surprise you to hear that I find myself longing for Rose Manor, especially now we're at the height of the season. I'm like my mother in that respect, I suppose."

The insight didn't surprise him at all, considering it fit perfectly with how he remembered her. "Does Hawthorne share your sentiments, I wonder? He has never concealed his preference for Town, nor does he seem particularly suited to the pastoral life."

Her expression shuttered. "Where Lord Hawthorne decides to settle is neither here nor there. He certainly has never made any complaints to me. *And* he's been a frequent guest of my aunt of late."

James didn't much doubt it. "That may be the case, but I hardly see Hawthorne slaving over his acres. Not with the veritable army of stewards he has at his beck and call."

"Oh?" Miranda raised her brows pointedly. "I'm terribly interested to hear what you base that opinion on. You and the viscount are hardly bosom beaus. In any event, you're one to talk. When did you last visit your family set in Kent?"

"We're discussing the viscount, not me, and one need not live in a man's pockets to ascertain his nature, Miranda. Hawthorne's about as predictable as a fairytale's ending. And you needn't be so defensive. I only wish to see to you happy."

"As I am not of your concern, I suggest you turn your attentions elsewhere. In fact, I'm surprised to see you at all. I doubt Lady Stanton would approve of you associating with the likes of me."

The offhand comment snagged his attention. "Why suddenly bring my stepmother into this? Has she had words with you?"

He wouldn't pass it by the witch.

Miranda swallowed. "It's nothing that everyone isn't already thinking. Besides, it's of no consequence."

No consequence, his arse!

"I will strangle her," James muttered before airing aloud, "What—pray tell—do you mean by 'what everyone is thinking'?"

"Isn't it obvious?" she shot back. "You're a sought-after earl, whilst I, the daughter of an officer. Decorated as the colonel may be, it's hardly an advantageous match from your standpoint. Not that I have such ambitions, of course," she hastened to add as she went to turn away.

But James wasn't having a bar of it. He grasped her hand and gently turned her back to face him.

"Of course," he echoed, searching her stony expression for any hint to what she was thinking and coming up empty. "But you do realize this is nonsense. Why, there's no such talk of you and the viscount."

"That's different. Lord Hawthorne may be in line to inherit, but it's our fathers' long-held association that secured the match."

He scowled.

She sounded as if the union was a foregone conclusion.

"If by that you mean the pairing is predictably convenient, then I concur," he said, matching her glare with one of his own.

As Miranda opened her mouth to reply, James caught sight of a phaeton coming upon them fast. Acting on instinct, he pulled her in close and out of harm's way.

She collided with his chest, her breath fanning across his cheek.

He inhaled.

She smelled of summer berries. Sweet and comfortingly familiar.

If only he could hold on to her forever. But seeing the danger had passed, he had no choice but to let her go.

Miranda stepped back and brushed down her skirt with shaky fingers.

"Are you hurt?" he asked, checking for any signs of injury.

She shook her head, refusing to meet him in the eye. "Shall we continue?"

She walked off as if nothing had happened.

James swallowed a sigh as he fell into line behind her.

He was a little shaken himself. If he hadn't spied that carriage in time...

The consequences didn't bear thinking about.

Lost in thought, he was startled when Miranda turned to him the instant they reached her conveyance. "You were at Westminster this afternoon, were you not?"

James nodded. "I came directly from there in fact."

"So tell me, how was my father's bill received?"

He hesitated, wanting to be truthful yet reluctant to disappoint her. "It certainly sparked debate," he settled with.

"I see."

He was afraid that she did in fact *see*. "The tide will surely turn though, once everyone is fully appraised of the particulars," he added on a hopeful note.

Her worried look didn't abate, though, and his fingers itched to smooth the fine lines from her brow.

Taking so much upon herself, it was a wonder she didn't cripple under all the weight.

"Mira—"

"Good grief!" Lucinda exclaimed, shattering the moment. "I saw absolutely everything and swear you were almost trampled to death right in the middle of Berkeley Square! How that poor excuse for a driver failed to see you defies explanation."

Miranda recovered first. "A slight exaggeration, don't you think, dearest? As you can see, we are unharmed, having had ample opportunity to move aside."

Lucinda slid James an appreciative look. "Only because of your quick reflexes, my lord."

Miranda snorted, but her expression was carefully blank as she held out her hand. "Good day, Lord Stanton. Thank you for seeing us safely to our carriage."

He clasped her hand and kissed it lightly. "Miss Drayton, it was an absolute pleasure as always."

She climbed into the carriage and scooted to the far end of the seat.

Blowing out his breath, James stepped aside.

"Miss Lucinda," he said, turning to assist her up.

Lucinda smiled. "I for one am anticipating our next encounter, Lord Stanton, as it's sure to be most edifying."

"I'll do my utmost to exceed your expectations, then."

James nodded to the coachman and watched the carriage take off, soon becoming lost to the afternoon traffic.

How long he stood there, he couldn't say.

A sharp elbow to his back brought him back to rights again.

"My apologies," he said to the disgruntled-looking fellow who'd bumped into him.

The man grunted and hurried on his way.

James shrugged and turned in the direction of Brook Street.

He'd dismissed his own carriage earlier, his townhouse but a few blocks away.

On the walk home, he was of two minds.

He'd managed to have a decent conversation with Miranda, which could only be considered progress. She mightn't have appreciated his criticism of Hawthorne, but she needed to hear it all the same. Continuing blindly down that path would only lead to heartache.

As much as Miranda may wish to deny it, she didn't desire the viscount. At least not in any true sense, which put James at a distinct advantage. He hadn't missed the catch to her breath when he'd pulled her out of the phaeton's path, nor how she trembled at his touch. Yet something was holding her back. Something besides the viscount. It was like she didn't trust her own feelings anymore—didn't trust *him* anymore. And until he regained that trust, he'd have no chance of winning back her heart. Of course, Muriel's interference wasn't exactly aiding his cause.

James walked into his townhouse and held on to his hat.

He recognized the look on his butler's face.

"Don't tell me my stepmother has returned, Benson."

If so, she was in for a rude awakening.

"No, not Lady Stanton, my lord. Lord Camden awaits you in the study, however."

James grinned. "That's all right, then."

He relinquished his hat and strode into his study, waving as Freddy made a half-hearted attempt to rise from the armchair facing the fireplace. "Pray, don't bestir yourself, Freddy. I can see you've made yourself right at home."

Freddy lifted his fork in salute before popping it into his mouth. "How is it I'm only now discovering your cook makes the best gooseberry pie in all of London? To think I considered us friends," he said between mouthfuls.

James rolled his eyes. "Mayhap that's because I know you too well." He looked to the half-empty glass on the side table. "And I see you've found my best brandy, too."

Freddy grinned. "You know, I do believe Benson has a soft spot for me."

"Humph," James sounded as he went to pour himself a drink. He then settled in the armchair perpendicular to his friend. "As much as I'm honored by the impromptu visit, I must say I'm surprised to see you this time of day. Surely you have some engagement or other to be getting to."

Freddy's smile disappeared. "Lady Fowler's ball, most unfortunately. There's no rush, though. Astoundingly, my sisters require no less than three hours to ready themselves of an evening. Not that I expect you'll be present to appreciate the bedazzling results, seeing a certain lady isn't billeted to attend this evening..."

James swirled the glass in his hand, refusing to rise to the bait.

"In all seriousness, James, what are you about?"

James raised his gaze and met his friend's piercing blue stare. "Can't a fellow court a lady without generating all this speculation?"

Freddy snorted. "When that fellow's made no secret of his disdain for the wedded state? Then no, I'm afraid not."

"That didn't seem to bother you the other evening, when you practically begged me to take one of your sisters off your hands."

"I made that suggestion in jest knowing you wouldn't seriously consider either of them. Just like I suspect you haven't properly thought this through."

James scowled. "I assure you that I have."

It was all he could think of, in fact.

Freddy raised his brows. "You know this all sparks of that incident a year or so back. When you and Worthington were tussling over that actress. Sabrina, wasn't it? Or was it Selena?"

"Serena, actually," James returned with a frown. "But I don't see how that could be relevant."

"Can't you? Remind me. How long after you succeeded in winning that fair maiden did you throw her over for the seafarer's widow, Mrs. Simpson? A wife's not so easy to discard as a mistress, you know."

"As if I would discard the woman that I—"

Freddy settled into his seat. "Pray continue, James. Don't hold back when things are just starting to get interesting. The woman that you—"

James got up and replenished his glass. He made a point of not offering Freddy the same courtesy.

He didn't return to his chair, either. Instead, he propped himself against the fireplace mantle and went on the defensive.

"I don't know why I should explain myself to you. You aren't a relation of the lady in question. Indeed, one might wonder why you've suddenly taken such an interest. Need I be worried?"

It was Freddy's turn to scowl. "Don't be more of a fool than you already are, Stanton. The lady's not the issue here, you are. Tell me this, then. Say you somehow manage to convince Miss Drayton to take you on. Just what do you plan on doing with her?"

Such a ridiculous question deserved no better treatment.

"I intend to keep her locked in my dresser if you must know. But don't despair, I'll ensure to let her out for Sunday services."

Freddy tutted. "That you could even make such a quip hardly convinces me of your sincerity, my dear chap."

James snapped. "Do you think I would embark on this course of action without deeply considering the matter? I've seen the best and worst of marriage as you well know. I'd hardly toss my independence away on just anyone. Furthermore, I'm not about to let that dimwit of a viscount wed Miranda when he could never love her as much as I do!"

"Feeling better now, James? With that finally off your chest?"

James snorted.

He didn't, actually.

He felt as if he'd been racked over a pile of hot coals only to be dragged right back through them again.

"You've achieved what you've set out to do this afternoon then, I take it."

Freddy put aside his plate and took to his feet. "No need to thank me. I'd best leave you to it if you're to have any hope of success at your godmother's house party next week. I doubt Hawthorne will give up the lovely Miss Drayton without a fight."

James shook his head. "Must you persist on stating the obvious?"

He wasn't truly miffed, though.

Freddy was only looking out for him in his own bumbling way. Friends tended to do that, which James could understand even if he didn't always appreciate it.

He stepped forward, and Freddy shook his outstretched hand.

"I'm looking forward to Hampshire as it's bound to prove—"

"Interesting, I'm sure." James completed for him.

"I'll see myself out." Freddy departed with a jaunty wave.

James took the seat his friend had vacated and stared into the empty grate.

Speaking of his godmother's house party brought to mind Miranda's odd reaction whenever the subject was raised. Considering her love of Rose Manor, James could only conclude that her sudden aversion had something to do with him. As such, he was glad he'd kept his intended attendance to himself. Otherwise, she might fashion some excuse and bow out last minute.

Freddy might act the fool at times, but he was correct on one front. James' grand plan required Miranda to be at the appointed place at the appointed time. He couldn't afford to leave their future to chance.

Fate had already proved too capricious for his liking.

14

An Unexpected Dip

Three days later, Miranda joined Lucinda and their parents in the family coach for the day's journey to Rose Manor.

Their mother had insisted on a few quiet evenings at home pre-departure, and whilst Lucinda had railed at missing Lady Fowler's masked ball, Miranda had been grateful for the reprieve.

Considering the incident in Berkeley Square, she hardly wished to 'accidentally' run into James at yet another event. She was still reeling from their last encounter, which had been way too close for comfort.

Not that she could fault him for saving her from that runaway carriage. No, her wayward response to being back in his arms was the issue.

It was only after considerable reflection that she'd concluded her reaction had to be the shock. The phaeton had come upon them so quickly, she hadn't the opportunity to brace for impact. And after finding herself literally abreast of James, was it any wonder her mind had taken her straight back to that night in her aunt's hallway?

It didn't mean anything, though. She was too sensible to think otherwise. So, some of her old feelings had resurfaced. She'd once loved James with the whole of her innocent heart, believing him her future, her destiny. It would've been more surprising if she'd felt nothing pinned in his embrace.

As much as she might wish it, she wasn't made of stone.

With that reasoning, she'd come to some level of acceptance. James was here for the interim and there was little she could do about it, save continue with her original plan. She would concentrate on the viscount and come away from her aunt's house party an affianced—no, make that a *happily* affianced—woman. Then that would be that.

She grunted, Lucinda elbowing her side as she leaned across her lap, the view obviously superior from Miranda's side of the carriage.

"Thank goodness, the end is nigh," Lucinda said as the signpost for Alton flew by. "The journey has taken absolutely *forever*, and I find myself oddly exhausted as a result."

The colonel peered over the papers he'd been studying and snorted. "Considering your infernal chatter, my girl, that's hardly surprising. I know I've aged twelve moons just listening to your nonsense!"

Lady Nora stirred from her doze and gave a sleepy blink. "Have we arrived?"

"Not yet," the colonel grumbled in response.

One would think after undertaking the exact same journey many times each year, they would be accustomed to it. However, it only seemed to bring out the worst in them.

It was fortunate Rebecca and Jonathan had remained in London this time around as all six Draytons confined to one carriage was never a pleasure ride.

Mercifully, Rose Manor lay just up ahead, and Miranda's heart lifted to see its familiar stone façade peeking through the trees.

As the carriage pulled to a stop at the top of the rise, the manor's front doors were flung wide. Aunt Bethel and Meg swept onto the portico; their faces alit in welcome.

After being let down from the carriage, Miranda joined her family on the front steps.

The Dowager Duchess extended a hand to her brother. "Good day, Richard. How was the journey? I see you made good time and look no worse for it."

"We Draytons are nothing but punctual, as you can surely attest. In saying that, the weather was on our side for once." The colonel bowed to kiss her hand then turned to Meg. "Good day, Mrs. Barlow. You look well."

Meg smiled, seemingly amused by the colonel's formal manner. "Thank you, Sir Richard. As always, we are pleased to welcome you all to our humble abode."

Meg had been the Dowager Duchess' trusted companion these fifteen years past, so was as much a fixture at Rose Manor as Aunt Bethel herself. In fact, Miranda couldn't remember a time when Meg wasn't in residence, and she embraced the comely widow with the same degree of affection as she did her aunt.

The Dowager Duchess ushered them into the manor's expansive front hall.

"Hurst has made up your usual rooms," she informed them, "and seeing you're the first to arrive, you have ample time to freshen up. A light repast will be served in the drawing room on the hour."

Her aunt ran her household as smoothly as a military operation. Just one of the many traits she shared with her younger brother, not that either would admit to the slightest commonality.

"Will there be cinnamon scrolls?" Lucinda turned to their aunt, ever hopeful.

The Dowager Duchess' eyes twinkled. "You never know..."

Lucinda squealed, then skipped up the stairs on the way to her room.

The colonel tracked her progress with a frown. "I don't know how I could have sired such a hoyden. Hours of tutelage gone to waste."

"Come now, Richard," Aunt Bethel said. "The dear child is merely enthusiastic, which I happen to find endearing."

He snorted before turning to his wife. "Shall we repair to our room, my dear?"

Lady Nora took his arm, and they headed up the stairs.

"And how are you, dearest?" The Dowager Duchess turned to Miranda.

Miranda smiled. "I'm a little fatigued from the journey. Otherwise, I'm very happy to be back at the manor."

"I'm so pleased to hear that," her aunt returned. "You know how Meg and I delight in having you, and if you hurry, you'll have time for a stroll in the garden before the great onslaught descends."

"As if I would ever deny myself the opportunity. I will see you later, then," she said, brushing a kiss across her aunt's cheek.

Hastening to her room, Miranda exchanged her dusty traveling clothes for a simple day dress. Back downstairs, she headed out the front door.

Once clear of the portico, she took the well-worn path down the side of the manor, which led to the expansive rose garden at the back.

Spying a bed of Old Blush, she paused to take in its scent. Then she hurried through the arbor—seeing no cause to linger there—and came to rest by the edge of the lake.

The water glistened beneath the setting sun, which had painted the horizon a pretty collage of orange and pink.

Taking to a bench in the shade, Miranda gave a contended sigh. Her aunt had timed the house party precisely when she'd needed it most.

She couldn't explain her affinity with Rose Manor, only that she always felt more at home here than in Town. Perhaps it was the quiet, calm acceptance of the place, where the lack of strictures allowed one a certain measure of freedom.

Looking down, Miranda spied a pile of discarded clothing and pair of dusty riding boots propped up against a nearby tree trunk.

Odd. No one was around.

Then a loud splash drew her attention back to the lake and she sucked in a breath as a familiar figure swam into view.

Merciful heavens, what in the world was James doing here?

A ridiculous question, of course. But would a bit of fore-warning been too much to ask? She'd left Town to escape the man, for goodness' sake!

Despite her discomfort she couldn't tear her gaze away, tracking his progress as he propelled himself through the crystal-clear waters.

To think she'd convinced herself that his return was of no consequence. The gods must be besides themselves in laughter, thinking her so deluded.

James paused and reached up to slick back his hair, the action causing his practically transparent shirt to pull tightly across his chest.

Miranda gasped and, seeing him turn in her direction, quickly leaned back into the shadows.

Too late.

James had caught her staring and was moving toward the shoreline, flicking water off his body as he went.

Dear Lord!

Miranda leaped to her feet.

She had to escape, yet she was incapable of moving. Even breathing had somehow become an insurmountable task.

James came to stand before her, and her throat went dry.

A droplet of water had escaped from his hair and was running down the right side of his face as if to mock her.

When it cleared his jawline and broached his neck, she snapped her gaze to his, where it would forever remain.

She'd seen plenty enough already.

"Miranda," he said, looking distinctly amused. "What's the matter? Afraid I'll drag you into the lake with me?"

Stepping back, she winced, the back of her knees colliding with the stone bench. "Ha! Afraid you'll drip all over my skirts, more like. Why are you here?"

He flashed a rakish grin. "I thought that obvious. Care for a dip? The water's lovely and you do look rather flushed."

"Certainly not!" she said, her cheeks blazing all the more. "Don't you have your own lake to dabble in—in *Kent*?"

"Why would I travel that far when all I could wish for is right here? And I must say, from this standpoint, one couldn't want for a better view."

Miranda couldn't speak—couldn't think—with him looking at her thusly. As if she were a tall glass of iced lemonade on a midsummer's day. Although icy was the last word she'd use to describe herself at that moment.

He reached out, and her eyes fluttered shut to feel his cool fingertips against her fevered cheek.

Without thought, she leaned into his caress.

Oh no, no, no. This wouldn't do at all!

James traced the smooth line of Miranda's jaw, marveling at the softness of her skin.

When he'd first spied her from the water, he thought he must be dreaming. Because for one gloriously unguarded moment there, her expression was so intense with longing, it tugged at him as surely as a seafarer's rope.

Unwilling to break the spell, he'd approached slowly, lest she bolt in panic. But against all expectation, she'd stayed, and he intended to make the most of whatever time she awarded him.

Of course, he hadn't planned on revealing himself in quite this manner.

Traveling by horseback, he hadn't hesitated, jumping in the lake to cool off before heading up to the house as he'd done many a time previously. Miranda stumbling across him mid-act was just a happy coincidence. And now she was here, with him, at their most favorite place, he could hardly be sorry.

He inched forward, his heart missing a beat to hear her staggered breath. To see the pulse fluttering wildly at the base of her throat.

"You are lovely," he said as she swayed closer.

Cradling her jaw with both hands, he dipped his head. But just as their lips were to meet, she drew back, slipping out of his grasp.

"You are here for the house party," she said, her lips settling into a firm line.

"Yes." He dropped his arms to his sides.

She cleared her throat. "I best leave you to make yourself presentable then. The other guests will be arriving soon." Her gaze started to blaze a trail down his body before she quickly averted her head with a moue of distress.

Probably for the best.

His damp clothing clung like a second skin, thus was unlikely to be hiding much, if anything at all.

Still, he couldn't let her run off without discussing their near-kiss. "Mira—"

But she was already edging away, waving her hand in a vague gesture. "Yes, I shall leave you to...it. I'm sure to see you at dinner."

Without awaiting an answer, she turned and hastened up the rise.

As he could hardly go after her given his current state, he consoled himself with the thought. Now at Rose Manor, he'd have plenty of opportunities to persuade Miranda to his way of thinking. And if the past few minutes were any indication, their future would be wondrously bright, albeit likely to conflagrate at a moment's notice.

But wouldn't they have fun dousing all the flames?

With a grin, he dived back into the lake. He'd be wise to dampen his ardor before presenting himself to his godmother.

Some anticipation for the house party was only to be expected. But it wouldn't do to appear *too* eager.

15

Flirtations and Fabrications

M iranda didn't look back. She dared not.

What an utter ninnyhammer!

James only had to touch her—and rather innocuously, at that—and she practically turned to pudding in his hands.

Clearly, she'd lost all sense. And if she didn't get ahold of herself, James would think she still had a tendre for him, which would be beyond insufferable. But the way his clothes had hugged his muscular form...

She refused to venture down that treacherous path again!

Rushing into the manor house, she almost collected her aunt in the hallway.

The Dowager Duchess frowned. "What is it, Miranda? You appear to have seen a ghost."

A devil more like, came her immediate thought. But she only voiced, "Nothing so terrifying as that, Aunt. Realizing the time, I was hurrying back to my room. Wouldn't want to be late for tea and leave all those cinnamon scrolls to Lucinda."

"I vow you and your siblings wouldn't visit half as much if it wasn't for Cook's scrolls," she said.

"You know that's not true. We adore you and Meg at least half as much."

"How nice it is to be appreciated, my dear. Now, tell me what truly has left you in such a tizz?"

Miranda sighed, deciding she had nothing to gain by prevaricating. "I didn't realize James would be attending this year."

Her aunt's lips split into a grin. "Marvelous, isn't it? Did you happen upon my wayward godson in the drive, perchance?" She looked to the door expectantly.

"You could say that. He is stabling his mount as we speak and is bound to be along presently." Miranda crossed her fingers at her slight stretching of the truth.

"I couldn't be more thrilled that he's finally come! Can you believe it's been years since he last visited us at the manor?"

Miranda flushed, accepting her part in his desertion as due.

If only she'd had more foresight, all this could've been avoided.

"I am sure you will delight in having him then, Aunt," she said.

"I expect we all shall. No one can deny the rogue's excessively diverting to have around. Why, the lad makes me feel years younger if not a day! With all you young things milling about the place, this is sure to be my most memorable house party yet."

Miranda didn't doubt it for a second. "I best get ready, then. Wouldn't want to tarnish the Drayton's unblemished record for punctuality. Father would never forgive me."

"No, we couldn't have that," the Dowager Duchess said with a smile.

Miranda restrained herself from fleeing up the stairs like the hounds of hell were nipping at her heels, but it was a close call. Knowing her luck, James would appear, and she needed time to recover. Several hours in the very least.

Inside her bedchamber, she collapsed against the solid hardwood door and closed her eyes.

You are lovely...

Miranda let the words brush over her skin like a warm summer's breeze, her fingers tracing the path he'd scorched down the side of her cheek.

Realizing what she was about, she snapped her hand back to her side.

Not so *lovely* to warrant any consideration these past three years, she reminded herself with a snort.

"Are you well, miss?" her maid, Abigail, asked from across the way.

Miranda's heart faltered.

She'd thought herself alone in the room.

Pushing away from the door, she looked to where Abigail was laying out her evening gown on the bed.

"I'm perfectly well," she said. "Indeed, I am eager for the festivities to begin. You know how my aunt lives to put her fellow hostesses to shame, her house parties having gained legendary status in our exalted circle."

She snapped her mouth shut to stop its blabbering.

"You'll be in good company then, miss," Abigail declared loyally. "And I've heard all the guests have arrived, so we best begin else you be late."

Miranda smothered a sigh as she moved to the stool behind the dresser. Abigail immediately set to work, addressing the mess that had become of her hair.

Watching the maid unravel her curls, Miranda wished she could untangle her thoughts as easily.

How in heaven's name was she to hold herself together for the duration of the house party?

As much as it pained her to admit, she still had a weakness when it came to James Stanton. And finding him at the lake all wet and looking so, well, *manly*, did little to mitigate the condition. Thanks to the near miss at Berkely Square, she knew exactly how his taut body felt pressed against her own. She grew edgy and tense just thinking about it.

She squirmed in her seat, only to still at her maid's sound of protest through the plethora of pins she held between her teeth.

"My apologies, Abigail," she said, firmly harnessing her thoughts.

From the looks of it, she had two options.

The first was to simply warn James off and demand he let her be. But then he would expect an explanation, and she could hardly say that simply being around him was hazardous to her frame of mind. She'd rather die!

The best she could come up with was to ignore James completely with the hope he would desist of his own accord. He must see her as some sort of challenge. There could be no other explanation. Unless he was so desperate for companionship, any female would suffice.

If she refused to engage, he'd soon lose interest and go chase easier pickings. And as an added deterrent, she'd stick to the viscount like Flanders glue. Failing that, her sister, or mother, indeed any of her aunt's guests. James could hardly prove tempting with a bevy of people acting as a buffer.

Miranda met her maid's gaze in the looking glass.

"There you are, miss, pretty as a picture," Abigail said as she applied the final touches.

Miranda examined herself in the mirror.

She looked perfectly poised, which was more than half the battle.

"Thank you, Abigail. You have outdone yourself once again."

Beaming, Abigail handed Miranda her shawl.

Wrapping the sheer cloth around her shoulders, Miranda made for the door. She descended the staircase and headed toward the hum of conversation stemming from the drawing room.

Pausing in the doorway, she could see she was the last to arrive.

Lord Sommerville, Lord Hawthorne, and Emily and Kit's father, Mr. Alfred Burton, were engrossed in conversation with her father by the fireplace.

Her mother was seated by Lady Moira Camden on the damask sofa, the pair looking set on becoming fast friends. Nearby, Freddie Camden and his sisters, the misses Annabel and Sarah, were exchanging pleasantries with her Aunt Bethel and Meg.

Lucinda had joined Emily, Kit, and Miss Primrose by the pianoforte, her sister's face animated as she spoke.

And last—but as he surely would argue, not least—was James, thankfully properly attired as he conversed with the late duke's good friends, the Lord and Lady Whincup, and the countess' brother, Lord Dunston.

Watching the merry quartet, Miranda stiffened as Lady Whincup leaned closer to James, gifting him an unhampered view of her generous bosom. James didn't even blink, murmuring something in return that earned him a rap of her fan.

Miranda huffed.

Clearly, she'd been worrying over naught. Far from seeking her out, James hadn't even noticed her presence in the room.

Inexplicably annoyed, she set a path for her sister, who was still engrossed in debate with the twins and Miss Primrose.

Lucinda stepped aside to make room for Miranda without a break in conversation.

"But surely, the Scarlet Lady's identity will be uncovered soon. She must be running out of disillusioned lovers to slay, and it's only a matter of time before someone makes the connection," she insisted, obviously referring to the latest installment of *Miss M's Mysteries*.

The Scarlet Lady was Emily's latest villainess, and it seemed half of society was up in arms trying to unmask her identity, Lucinda being on the forefront.

Kit nodded to Miranda in greeting before responding. "I wouldn't be so quick to assume, Miss Lucinda. *Miss M's* fictional world seems to mirror that of our own, where the majority only see what they wish to see, remaining blissfully ignorant of the rest."

Emily laughed. "What a profound yet utterly depressing take on society, brother dear. But then, you spend most of your days lurking around courtrooms, so it's not surprising that you've become jaded as a result. What say you, Mira?" she asked, turning her sparkling gaze to Miranda. "Do you think Lucinda has the right of it? That the Scarlet Lady would be so foolish to make a mistake that leads to her exposure?"

Miranda returned her amused look. Emily was the only person who could possibly know the answer. Nevertheless, it was diverting to play along. "Who's to say what anyone would do in the throes of passion. One is hardly equipped with forward thinking in such a state."

Miss Primrose nodded. "Whilst I'm not convinced *Miss M's Mysteries* is appropriate reading material for proper young ladies, I must agree with Miss Drayton. The truth has a way of getting out, regardless how desperately one tries to conceal it."

The dinner bell sounded then, bringing an auspicious end to the discussion.

Lucinda moved to the door. "Thank goodness. All this talk of intrigue has left me quite ravenous, especially as my aunt's promised cinnamon scrolls were nowhere to be found."

Miranda smiled and went to follow her sister and the others to the dining room. She stopped short of the door, the viscount bowing before her.

"Good evening, Miss Drayton," he said. "May I have the pleasure of escorting you to dinner?"

Miranda laid her hand on his arm. "You certainly may, Lord Hawthorne. I'm glad to see you arrived safely. How did you enjoy the journey?"

"The roads were entirely passable, so we made good time. I take your journey was similarly uneventful?"

"Oh, most assuredly. My father wouldn't allow for anything less. I even had time to visit the gardens before coming down to dinner."

Lord Hawthorne led her into the hall, and they paused outside the dining room door. "Would you care for another stroll after dinner? As I recall, the grounds here are beyond compare, so I wouldn't mind revisiting them myself. If you are not too fatigued from the journey, that is."

Miranda quickly obliged as the request fell entirely into her plans. "I would be happy to accompany you, my lord. My aunt's gardens are only the more spectacular by night."

16

Discord on the Menu

Now James knew his godmother prided herself on setting a fine table, but she'd truly outdone herself that evening.

The colossal oak dining table was draped in a crisp, white linen, the rose centerpieces providing a vibrant contrast to the plain backdrop. The duchy's custom-made porcelain proudly marked each place, its accompanying silverware buffed to a high shine. Not to be outshone were the five footmen positioned against the back wall, each holding a covered platter, the smells from which providing a tantalizing hint of what was to come.

Approaching the table, James' enthusiasm for the meal dipped once he discovered how far he'd been set from Miranda. Then his appetite vanished altogether to see Hawthorne assist Miranda into her chair and take the place beside her. With Dunston seated to her other side, she'd be lucky to make it through the first course without falling asleep in her turtle soup.

Pushing aside his disgruntlement, James held out a chair to Lady Whincup and mustered a smile. When he saw Freddy's sister Annabel had been seated to his right, his smile turned genuine.

He swept out her chair with a flourish. "How lucky you are, Annie my girl, to be granted the best seat in the house."

Annabel rolled her eyes. "You clearly haven't lost your inflated sense of self-importance, my lord. And that's 'Miss Camden' to you. We're in company, in case you hadn't noticed."

James grinned and took his seat. "It's been so long, I'm afraid I'm in need of the reminder. How fortunate you are here then, *Miss Camden*, to keep me on the straight and narrow."

If he couldn't sit by Miranda, Freddy's sister would be his second choice. Having known her almost as long as Miranda, he considered Annabel easy company.

Lady Whincup, however, was likely to pose more of a problem.

Catching wind of their conversation, she veered closer. "If you're in want of assistance, Lord Stanton, I'm at your disposal. Society is difficult to navigate at the best of times, let alone when one's been removed for so long. Why, you might make a terrible *faux pas*, talking to the wrong person for instance, and we couldn't have that."

James covered up Annabel's snort by saying, "How kind of you to offer, Lady Whincup, though I hardly deserve the consideration. If I happen to misstep, I have no one but my-self to blame. In fact, some might consider it fair punish-ment for my past misdeeds."

"You're too hard on yourself, my lord," she returned with a simper. "What you need is to surround yourself with friends who'll champion your cause. And I'd be happy to lead the charge, seeing I've a feeling we're destined to be the best of friends."

James was poised to correct the notion, but he found Mi-randa looking his way, so he extended his lips into a smile. "I would like that."

Lady Whincup fluttered her lashes and leaned so far for-ward, her enormous bosom threatened to spill into his lap. "Then we're in perfect accord."

Suppressing a shudder, James looked back to Miranda.

Her grip had tightened around her wineglass, so he lifted his own in silent toast. Having no option but to follow, she took her glass to her lips, her eyes murderous as she drank.

James mirrored the action, downing his whole glass.

Now she had an inkling of what it was like to be in his shoes.

After everything that had happened, she could at least acknowledge his existence. Or had he imagined the liquid pool of desire in her eyes when they'd almost kissed that very afternoon?

The first course arrived then, and dinner passed by in a blur, James upping Lady Whincup's outrageous comments with another of his own.

He couldn't resist. Not when the action seemed to provoke Miranda no end.

By the conclusion of the meal, James was relieved when his godmother led the ladies out the room, leaving the men to their port.

Who'd have thought feigning interest in someone would prove so taxing?

Nevertheless, with the ladies gone, he found himself watching the clock. So he suggested that they hurry their port and return to the parlor, Hawthorne surprisingly seconding the notion.

Whilst having little respect for the man, James wasn't about to look a gift horse in the mouth, and he led the way back to the rest of their party. As soon as he stepped into the drawing room, though, Lady Whincup cornered him, leaving Miranda wide open, and it wasn't long before Hawthorne had Miranda on his arm and was escorting her out to the terrace.

No wonder the cur had been so keen to return.

James hid a scowl, turning to Lady Whincup at the tug of his sleeve.

"How refreshing to find a man who doesn't linger on his port, my lord," she said, offering up what he supposed she considered a sultry smile. "Or may I call you James?"

"Oh, but that would be entirely too familiar. Wouldn't you agree, Lady Whincup?" he said, inching away.

The countess dropped her lower lip and held on all the tighter. "Nonsense. We've already agreed to be friends, have we not? Besides, don't you think we owe it to our hostess to ensure her party is a success? And what better way to achieve that than by leaving Rose Manor better acquainted than when we first arrived."

"Perhaps we should pose the question to Lord Whincup. He's always seemed the reasonable sort."

Surely, the mention of her husband would temper her fervor.

"I wouldn't even bother," she said, trilling a laugh. "Stuart only cares for his investments and horseflesh where everything else lies beneath his notice. Hence, he and my brother get along so well."

Lord save him from neglected wives and all that entailed. "Be that as it may, we can hardly claim to be that close of acquaintances."

"An oversight that can easily be rectified," Lady Whincup countered, brazenly stroking his arm.

James shrugged off her hand.

He should have known better than to encourage her in the first place.

"I must see to my godmother as I've yet to pay my respects. If you would excuse me, madam."

He took his leave before Lady Whincup could even think of protesting, straightening his sleeves as he went. He veered off to the terrace and went straight to the balustrade.

The Dowager Duchess must've witnessed his deflection for she appeared shortly thereafter.

"Should they be out in the dark without a chaperone?" James demanded without preamble, tracking the cozened couple strolling the gardens.

His godmother laughed. "Heavens, James, I would never have taken you for such a stickler. What could be the harm, hmmm? They are within clear sight of the house and my niece has a sensible head on her shoulders."

"It's not your niece's head that I'm worried about," he muttered. "And 'in clear sight' is rather debatable, don't you think? Hawthorne could pull Miranda into the shadows at any moment!"

The Dowager Duchess gave an arched look. "Well, I suppose you'd know more about these things than I. Even so, with you acting as her sentinel, our girl's virtue is surely safe. Why are you so concerned?"

He crossed his arms. "I'm not concerned so much as cautious. I consider Miranda family, thus I'm looking to her welfare as I would my own stepsisters."

His godmother patted his shoulder. "Keep telling yourself that if it helps. But if you want Miranda for yourself, I wouldn't tarry if I were you, otherwise you're in real danger of losing out."

She then swept back into the house, leaving James to stew on her parting remark.

Miranda and Hawthorne disappeared down a darkened path, and his frown deepened.

His godmother's advice was easier said than done.

How difficult it was to pursue someone when they were so blastedly intent on another.

17

Moonlight Encounters

As Lord Hawthorne led her down the lantern-lit garden path toward her aunt's towering statue of Aphrodite, Miranda tried not to be discouraged. No easy task considering, since stepping off the terrace and into the most romantic of settings—a rose garden by moonlight, for goodness' sake—their conversation hadn't ventured far from the mundane. From the unseasonably mild weather to the health of their respective families, then on to the Dowager Duchess' upcoming plans for the visit.

Not once had they delved into more meaningful territory, nor had there even been a hint of a potential future between them. At this rate, Miranda might become a viscountess within the next decade or so, but only if she were truly fortunate.

They continued to meander through the garden, Lord Hawthorne making no move to press closer let alone attempt a kiss. Apart from absently patting her hand at one point, he acted as if they were mere acquaintances, and rather distant ones at that.

Miranda was beginning to wonder why he even suggested the stroll.

To compound matters further, she couldn't shake the feeling that they were being watched. If their clandestine voyeur hoped to catch them in a compromising position, however, he or she was bound to come away disappointed. Unless she could somehow angle for a kiss.

She didn't stop to question why it had suddenly become imperative that the viscount kissed her. Only if he did kiss her, a proposal would surely follow. Then all the waiting would be over, and they could get on with the rest of their lives.

With that purpose in mind, she gazed to the heavens. "What a delightful evening it is! I've never seen so many stars, nor the moon so bright."

The viscount didn't even spare an upwards glance. "The sky's always clearer in the country, away from the dirt and soot of Town, you see."

Miranda's shoulders slumped.

That was that then. She just wasn't the passion-inspiring type.

Although James certainly seemed tempted at the lake earlier.

She immediately ousted the ridiculous thought.

James didn't count. He wasn't exactly discerning. One only had to look at Lady Whincup, though Miranda wished she'd never set eyes on the jade. The way she'd salivated over James through dinner had been nothing short of nauseating. In fact, the behavior only reminded Miranda of a certain widow from years gone by.

No wonder she was feeling so out of sorts.

But all that didn't detract from the fact that she herself was lacking in some way. She was incapable of attracting the *right* sort of gentleman. Clearly, lovemaking was not her forte, and mayhap she'd been too hasty refusing Lucinda's offer to lend one of her books. She could well do with all the help she could get!

Miranda started when the viscount suddenly stopped to ask, "We are friends, are we not?"

Blinking, she quickly returned, "Undoubtably, my lord."

"And our temperaments well aligned, don't you think?"

"Again, yes, I believe that to be the case."

She sidled closer. Surely, he would kiss her now.

"Excellent." He stepped back and reclaimed her arm. "With that settled, we best head back to the manor before we are missed."

Miranda shook her head and followed along blindly.

That was it?

She hadn't expected any grand declaration of love, but a little wooing wouldn't have gone astray.

Curiously, the lack of such in their courtship to date hadn't bothered her until recently, and she frowned to think the alteration had something to do with the man currently standing on the terrace glowering down at them.

"Stanton," Lord Hawthorne said stiffly, bringing them to a stop at the base of the steps.

"Viscount, Miss Drayton. How did you find the gardens?" James' lazy drawl contrasted against the gaze he had leveled on them, which was as hard as flint.

Miranda tossed her head. "Why, with the stars so dreamy and the heady scent of roses permeating the air, we couldn't have asked for a more magical evening."

She smiled to see the tick that appeared on James' cheek in response.

She was not about to let him intimidate her. They'd done no wrong, the viscount going so far as to secure her father's permission before they even stepped foot on the terrace.

Lord Hawthorne started up the stairs. "We were just heading in, Stanton. If you would care to excuse us."

But James held fast to his position, leaving them no option but to go around him. "I'm sure Miss Drayton would prefer to linger, considering it's such a fine evening and all. Feel free to leave us, though, Hawthorne, if you're needed elsewhere."

Miranda didn't appreciate her wishes being discussed as if she wasn't present.

She opened her mouth in protest but feeling Lord Hawthorne stiffen beside her, she decided to let him issue James the set down he deserved.

However, the viscount only said, "Very well," then gave *her* a speaking look in parting.

It was lowering to think she was scarcely worth the effort.

Without looking at James, Miranda stormed off to the far corner of the terrace.

Considering her current state, she couldn't rule out bloody murder, and she wouldn't want to scandalize her aunt's guests so early in the piece. The leisurely pace with which James followed didn't aid his cause either.

"What is the meaning of this, my lord?" she hissed when he was within striking distance. "I have no desire to converse with you privately. Talk with you at all, in fact."

"It's James, by the by, and why ever not, Miranda?" he asked mildly.

She curled her fingers into a fist. "*Because* we have nothing to discuss. Surely that's reason enough."

"I happen to disagree. We are friends, or at least we were at one time. And friends look out for each another, do they not?"

Miranda was flabbergasted. He lost claim to his 'friend' title long ago. "You cannot amble your way back and expect everything to be just as you left it. The world doesn't operate that way."

"I do realize that. But by the same token, it's impossible to erase the past as if it had never been. All the fun times we had, our adventures in the woods, the long afternoons we spent frolicking by the lake, playing shuttlecock *there* yonder. You cannot tell me you don't remember."

Miranda closed her eyes. It would be much easier if she could forget.

Sensing James was edging closer, she jerked her eyes open and went to go around him. "Of course, I remember. But that was then, and this is now. We're no longer children, James."

"Don't I know it." He looked grim as he stepped into her path. "Did he kiss you, Miranda?"

She gasped.

As if he had the right to ask.

She moved backwards, coming to an abrupt halt when the railing found her back. She lifted her chin. "No...I mean...*yes*! Yes, he did, indeed!"

James stepped closer and clutched the railing to the either side of her shoulders, trapping her within the circle of his arms. "And how did you find him? Disappointing, I'd wager."

Miranda squeezed her eyes shut, wishing the dratted viscount had indeed gone and kissed her. Then she could've thrown the exact opposite straight back into James' face!

A shadow passed over her closed lids, and her breath caught, the slight movement of air against her cheek her only warning.

"We cannot have you left wanting," he murmured before his lips descended to hers.

She couldn't move, couldn't think. Only feel as his lips swept over hers, again, then again, and again. She grasped his arms as a long-buried, hot, tingly feeling washed over her, threatening to sweep her away.

He backed her further into the balustrade, and she shuddered to feel his intense heat pressed against her body. Against the full length of her body. With sudden panic, she pushed at his chest.

This was exactly what she must avoid!

James didn't budge.

Looking up, his expression was one of such wonder that she stilled.

He reached out and grasped a tendril of her hair, twisting it around his finger. With a gentle tug, he angled her head just so before slowly closing in on her once more.

She lifted her chin and met him halfway.

Just once more, she promised herself.

Then all was lost. Well and truly lost.

"Open for me, love," he rasped against her lips.

Refusal didn't even cross her mind.

He moaned—or was it she? It hardly mattered in any case.

He moved his hands to her waist, and she pushed up on to her toes, fisting the lapels of his coat. When he took her bottom lip into his mouth and suckled in the most sinful way imaginable, she let out a groan so wanton, the sound had her rearing back.

What the blazes did she think she was she doing?

Nothing good, that was plain.

She pushed him away, needing the space to breathe.

He muttered a curse and took a step back.

"Whatever do you want with me, James?" she said, raising her hand as a precaution.

He raked his fingers through his hair. "I'm surprised you even have to ask."

Miranda sucked in a breath. "Well, I don't care for your games. Why not go and practice your wiles on someone else? I'm sure Lady Whincup would be only too happy to oblige."

He stilled.

He didn't much like having his behavior called in to question, did he?

"You have it all wrong. I'm not *toying* with you, Mira. I would never even entertain the notion. Besides, you've no reason to be jealous of—"

"Jealous? Who's *jealous*? My goodness, I don't know where my head was at. I hardly think this..." She waved her hands between their bodies in a sweeping motion. "...is wise. We wouldn't want any undue speculation now, would we?"

Heavens, if anyone had happened upon them only moments before, speculation wouldn't have even factored into the equation!

"They'd be no speculation as I wouldn't allow it. I'd mar—" He cut himself off.

"You'd what? Marry me?" Miranda gave a harsh laugh. "What a great honor you bestow me, my lord, being so willing to sacrifice yourself to save my reputation. Lucky for you, I wouldn't marry you even...*even* if the colonel had a pistol to my back!"

James looked about as stunned as she felt hearing her hateful words echoing back to them.

She didn't recognize this shrew she'd turned into, nor did she much like her.

With a wretched cry, she marched away before more vitriol could escape.

18

The Repercussions

Watching Miranda storm off, James let a string of curses fly. He'd well and truly bollocksed that up, and then some!

If only he could go back to that moment before he shot everything to pieces, then he wouldn't have left Miranda with any doubt. Far from kissing her on a *whim*, he'd kissed her because he couldn't survive another second without kissing her. That and the thought of Hawthorne laying so much as a finger on her had sent him a little crazed.

Hawthorne was no match for her, and he was bedeviled that Miranda refused to see it.

So, what better way to convince her than by showing her. When they came together, magic happened. Stars exploded, mountains collapsed, and all other manner of things cataclysmic. In fact, he'd been so struck by the feel of her lush lips, her fevered skin—hell, the feel of her whole body pressed against his—he'd almost collapsed to his knees and professed his eternal devotion then and there.

But he hadn't, baulking at the crucial moment. Seeing her closed expression, he'd been afraid she'd reject him outright.

Coward.

Annoyed with himself, he spun on his heels and strode into the starry night. He was in no condition to return to the drawing room in any event.

He took the path to the lake at a fast clip and stopping at the edge, he eyed the calm waters.

He'd fully expected Miranda's anger after his poor performance at dinner. What he'd failed to appreciate was the extent it would wound her, which was painfully evident in her speech as she railed at him.

Merde.

If only he hadn't left it so long, she wouldn't distrust him so.

How ironic that whilst he'd been gallivanting around the seedier parts of London, thinking to prove to himself that he needed no one, Miranda was back here doing much the same, learning to live without him. And by the looks of it, she'd done the much better job, having promoted him to the top of her 'Do Not Marry' list.

Looking to the lake, James considered tossing his sorry arse straight into it. But he had to return to the drawing room at some point—if only to reassure himself of Miranda's welfare—and he didn't think his godmother would appreciate him dripping pond water all over her Turkish pile.

So he turned back to the manor with the hope he'd expended enough foolishness for one evening.

Back in the parlor, Miranda only wished she could leave again. But after spending so long in the garden—with *both* the viscount and James—she had no option but to bide her time with the hope of dispelling any notions of impropriety. Regardless of how well deserved.

She couldn't think of what happened outside without her cheeks burning up, so she refused to even consider it. She sought out Emily and her sister as a means of distraction. There was plenty time for self-recriminations later in the privacy of her room.

Reaching her sister's side, Lucinda looked her over. "Well, did he kiss you?"

Miranda felt all her color drain from her face. Then she saw Emily's arched look and realized her sister was referring to the viscount, not James. *Obviously.*

She shook her head. Though, with her cheeks sizzling with heat again, her expression may have told a different story.

"Personally, I am more interested in what happened with Lord Stanton seeing he's yet to return from the terrace," Emily said.

Miranda refused to glance at her fiendishly perceptive friend.

"What's this about James?" Lucinda asked, raising her brows. "You don't have an earl and a viscount vying for you, do you, Mira? For that would be delicious, if so."

Miranda was quick to stamp out that notion. "Don't be ridiculous! Lord Stanton's practically family. You were only saying as much the other day."

She chose to ignore the snide voice in her head reminding her of precisely how *familiar* she and James were.

"But he's not truly family, is he?" Emily said with a smile.

"I hardly think… Oh, don't you start!" Miranda said, turning on her friend.

Kit came upon them with the sisters Annabel and Sarah on his arm. "What havoc are you raising now, sister dearest," he directed at Emily.

Emily pursed her lips, and regretting her outburst, Miranda answered him lightly, "A friendly difference of opinion. Nothing to be concerned about."

Thankfully, Kit let the subject slide. He turned to Annabel and Sarah. "I brought these delightful ladies over as they're of a mind to visit the village tomorrow. That way, you ladies will be happily entertained whilst we men are out fishing for your supper."

Annabel and Sarah nodded as they smiled back at Kit.

Lucinda frowned at them for a moment then her expression cleared. "What a splendid notion! Let's put the idea to my aunt at once." She linked her arms with the sisters and drew them away. "Hart's Drapery is an absolute marvel, their fabrics being second to none…"

Kit watched them go. "Your sister's something else, isn't she?"

Miranda chuckled. "You don't know the half of it." She then included Emily as she asked, "How have you settled into the manor? Are your rooms to your liking?"

Emily answered first. "Most definitely Ours has the most picturesque view of the garden."

Emily and her companion, Amy, had been allotted the green room, which overlooked the rose garden to the lake beyond. A vista which encompassed the rose arbor, although Miranda was grateful her friend failed to mention that particular aspect.

Kit confirmed that he too was well accommodated, and just as Miranda went to ask about the fishing expedition, she caught sight of James reentering the room. Then the grandfather clock in the hall struck twelve.

The words in her mouth drained away along with the surrounding air, her eyes flaring as they collided with James'.

From his look, he must've been remembering as she, and when he made a move in her direction, she felt herself pale.

She clutched her stomach, trying to quell its sudden upset.

She couldn't face James now. Not when she was feeling so *exposed*.

"Miranda? Miranda!" Emily called her name, so she mumbled something reassuring in return.

James was halfway across the room when the Dowager Duchess' pronouncement forestalled him.

Cards would be held over to the following evening so they could rest in preparation for the busy days ahead.

If James looked back, Miranda didn't notice, as she was already well on her way out the door.

19

Thorny Revelations

Miranda left her room early the next morn in search of her aunt. It wasn't like she could sleep for agonizing over last night's Huge Mistake—Huge *Mistakes*, rather.

One kiss could be excused considering James had taken her completely unawares. But to come back a second time... That suggested a susceptibility she didn't wish to entertain.

Despite the lapse, absolutely nothing had changed.

She would marry Lord Hawthorne, and *his* lips were the ones she'd be chasing from now on.

There would be no more kissing James Stanton! Never mind how tempting, all-consuming, and altogether too tantalizing his kisses may be. For they only led to a world of pain as she knew full well.

She descended the stairs, crossed the hallway to the grandfather clock and faced the girl she used to be.

That girl had been foolish, lost in a fairytale of her own making. But staring into her reflection, Miranda could see her eyes were now wide open.

Valiant knights didn't exist, and she certainly was no defenseless maiden in need of saving. She was completely in charge of her fate.

Turning toward the parlor, she followed the delicious smells emanating from inside.

"Cinnamon scrolls!" She hurried over to the couple seated at a covered table by the French doors.

"And a very good morn to you too, niece." Her aunt chuckled, offering her cheek for Miranda's ready kiss. She waved to an adjacent seat. "Join us while the buns are still warm."

Miranda sat, smiling when Meg held out the plate of scrolls.

"Still an early riser, I see," Meg commented.

Miranda took a pastry and bit into it with relish. "I see no point squandering the best part of the day lying in bed when there are plenty more interesting things to be doing with one's time," she said between swallows.

"I don't know," James aired from somewhere close behind. "I could name many a thing that would happily keep me abed all day."

Miranda breathed in sharply and coughed after inhaling an unhealthy portion of cinnamon in the process.

"You and your cheek." The Dowager Duchess tutted at James. "You've almost given poor Miranda here an apoplexy!" She passed a cup to Miranda. "Here, dearest."

Miranda accepted the tea whilst her aunt dealt with her godson. "We're surprised to see *you* so early, my boy. Even as a lad, I don't believe you ever graced us with your presence much before noon."

James took on a rueful look and sat beside Miranda. "Heaven help if I ever become that predictable, Godmother. Besides, if I'd remained abed, I would have missed having you three lovely ladies all to myself." He turned to Miranda, offering her the plate. "Would you care for another?"

Miranda took the first pastry that came to hand and set it down on her plate. "You just wanted your fill before everyone else surfaced."

"Ah, Mira," he said, selecting the largest scroll for himself. "As usual, you appear to know me better than I do myself." He bit into his pastry. "Hmm, delicious. Certainty worth the wait."

Miranda tore her eyes from his mouth and took another gulp of tea.

Best she quit the room right away.

After dispensing with his scroll, James' arm brushed hers on his way to another. She surged to her feet, collecting the edge of the table on the assent.

He immediately followed her up.

The Dowager Duchess and Meg looked over in surprise.

"Are you well, dear? You appear quite flushed all a sudden," her aunt said.

"Um, yes, I'm well." Miranda attempted to smooth her expression. "I just thought I'd take a stroll in the gardens now I've finished. If you don't mind, Aunt."

"Of course, I haven't an objection. In fact, if you could collect some roses as you go, I'd be most obliged. I require several large bunches to adorn the picnic tables this afternoon."

"Consider it done." Miranda welcomed the task as it would distract her from her thoughts.

"And James could help," her aunt continued.

"That won't be necessary—"

"I would be delighted—" James said at the same time.

The Dowager Duchess beamed at them. "Wonderful. That's settled then."

Meg brought her napkin to her mouth to cover her mirth.

"After you," James said, waving his free hand, his half-eaten scroll clutched in the other.

Miranda pasted on a smile and proceeded him from the room, her lips firming into a line the minute she entered the hall.

She couldn't believe she'd gotten herself into this predicament. Far from staying away from James, she now had to spend more time with him, alone, in the garden of all places!

She left him to finish his breakfast, heading upstairs to collect her bonnet and pelisse. She took her time. Not because she was preening, but in the hope James would become bored and go pester someone else.

When she returned, though, James was exactly where she'd left him. Except now he had an empty basket swinging from the hand where his pastry had been.

She descended the staircase, and her heart made a strange series of flips to find him watching her. The blasted, treacherous organ.

She hurried past the grandfather clock, not wanting to draw attention to it.

James seemed amused by her haste but thankfully kept his comments to himself. Instead, he stretched the basket toward her like a peace offering. "The housekeeper found you this. There's a pair of gloves and some secateurs inside."

Miranda thanked him and took the basket, being mindful to avoid all perilous hand contact in the exchange.

He opened the front door and waved her through. "Shall we?"

But the gap was too slight. Miranda had to hold her breath to avoid brushing against his coat on her way past.

Once clear, she crossed the portico and came to a stop by the front steps, the sun's reflection off the marble tiles momentarily blinding her.

James plowed into her from behind.

"Easy," he murmured, reaching out to steady her.

She quivered to feel his breath against her neck.

Jerking out of his grasp, she started down the steps as quickly as she could manage. "Glorious, is it not? The garden's so pretty this time of day."

"Yes, utterly breathtaking."

Her skin heated to hear the warm undertone to his voice.

Picking up her pace, she tore down the side path.

With any luck she'd lose him somewhere along the way.

James matched her stride for stride. "I must confess I regret not visiting more often, especially now I've returned."

"Aunt Bethel has certainly felt your absence," she returned tersely. "She loves you like a son, you know."

"You are correct, of course, and I cannot offer a valid excuse for staying away for so long."

Miranda stalled.

She hadn't expected such an admission.

"You won't hear any arguments from me, but I wouldn't go quite as far to say you had *no* justification."

James looked set to disagree, so she set off again, wishing she'd never pursued the topic in the first place. But he caught her by the arm, giving her no choice but to look at him.

"None of this was of your doing, Mira. I think it's past time we discussed what happened that Yuletide, don't you? But first—" He dropped his hand and swallowed. "Allow me to apologize for last night."

"There's no need to apologize," Miranda put in quickly, averting her gaze. "We both weren't at our best last evening, so let's blame our momentary madness on the moonlight, shall we? Besides, 'tis already all forgotten."

"My memory's not so defective as it turns out, but I'll let that slide for the moment. However, if last night isn't up for discussion, then I insist we talk about the kiss which started all this."

"No!" Miranda drew in a quick breath before continuing more evenly. "Rather, whatever could be gained from rehashing that old history? I once threw myself at you—to my instant regret, I must say—and you were well within your rights to be appalled by my behavior. End of story."

There. She'd admitted her failing—in a perfectly calm and reasonable manner too.

James was all astonishment, however. "That's not how I recall it at all. I was momentarily taken aback, yes—I hardly expected to come upon you in the hallway, let alone have you kiss me with such—but never was I appalled. Quite the opposite, in fact."

As if she wanted him softening the blow out of pity. "There's no need to spare my feelings, James. It happened a long, *long* time ago, and I'm well past that foolish flight of fancy, you can rest assured."

"If that's truly the case, then I'm not the least reassured, because I'm certainly not. Past it, that is."

Miranda slowly shook her head.

It couldn't be true as it went against everything that she remembered.

She looked past his shoulder and caught sight of the rose arbor in the distance—a clear omen if ever there was one.

She pursed her lips and faced him squarely. "Indeed? You had an odd way of showing it at the time. Which has no bearing whatsoever as the kiss was a mistake, just like the one last night. I'm to marry the viscount, and that's all there is to it. And if you have any respect for our past friendship, I would appreciate if you kept this conversation to yourself."

James looked mightily offended. "As if I would bandy about anything that happened between us in private, Miranda. Exactly what kind of man do you take me for?"

"A man who takes his pleasures where he wills, giving little thought to the consequences!"

With that said, she strode away.

20

A Plan Revised

Miranda didn't see Lucinda and Emily until she almost careered into them in the hallway.

"Whatever has you fleeing like a pack of wolves were on your tail?" Emily asked, peering at the open doorway.

Miranda flushed. "I was hardly running. It's a bit warm out, so I decided to return to the manor for a spell."

Lucinda looked at her oddly, but only said, "Well, we were coming to find you. Aunt Bethel told us of your assignment, and seeing we'd had our fill of scrolls—"

"More than our fill, in some cases," Emily inserted wryly.

"We took it upon ourselves to assist," Lucinda continued as if Emily hadn't spoken. She looked pointedly at Miranda's basket. "And how fortunate for you that we did, seeing you've yet to pick a bloom."

Miranda dropped her gaze, only just remembering the basket she held in the crook of her arm. "I was heading out the back," she improvised. "That's where the best varieties are located, as you may recall. Let's go that way, shall we?"

She started down the hall toward the lessor-used rear exit with her sister and Emily following behind.

Stepping outside, Lucinda looked to the garden. "Whatever's happened to James? We thought he was with you."

She made it sound as if Miranda had discarded him in a bush of some sort.

If only it were that simple.

"Er, he became tired of the task and went to see to his horse instead. He didn't exactly accompany me by choice," Miranda said, heading for the large bed of pink and white Alba roses to her left, shears at the ready.

When Lucinda and Emily joined her, she asked, "Did our aunt happen to mention her plans for the afternoon?"

"'Tea by the Lake' as I understand it. Hence, the need for all these roses you were supposedly collecting," Lucinda said.

Miranda ignored the jab and followed Emily to the sizable bush bursting with blooms of the deepest burgundy hue imaginable.

Emily bent closer. "What are these? For they smell divine."

"They're commonly known as Old Velvet," Miranda informed her, cutting several stems and adding them to the basket, removing any thorns as she went.

Lucinda snatched one of the roses from Miranda's grasp and proceeded to twirl the stem between her fingertips. "I fear a confession is in order, Mira. You are not, perchance, *a covert rosarian*?"

Miranda snorted. "Hardly. But when one spends so much time with our aunt, it would be impossible to come away without some of her horticultural knowledge rubbing off on one."

Besides, following *that* Christmas, Miranda had taken herself to the library and consumed all manner of subjects that had absolutely no relation to James Stanton, her aunt's extensive collection on rose cultivation seeming as good a read as any.

Lucinda grinned. "I wouldn't know about that. Botany isn't exactly my strong suit, and I spend at least as much time as you do with Aunt Bethel."

"That's because your head's always up in the clouds," Miranda said.

"I always thought it was off with the faeries," Emily added in much the same vein.

Lucinda brought her hands to her hips. "I'm standing right here, you do realize!"

Miranda and Emily burst into giggles. Lucinda shook her head then joined in the laughter.

The minutes passed pleasantly then, the trio chatting happily until the basket was overflowing. With their task complete, they started back to the manor.

Miranda paused by the steps. "I am glad that you sought me out because I could really use your help."

"Being your apprentice gardeners wasn't enough for you, then?" Lucinda said, her look sobering to see Miranda's expression. "Anything, Mira. You needn't even ask."

"I wish to secure a private moment with the viscount this afternoon and was hoping you could distract James in the meantime."

Curiosity pinched Emily's features. "You think Lord Stanton would interfere?"

Miranda shrugged even as she felt her cheeks heating. "I cannot be certain, of course. But considering his behavior of late, it's a distinct possibility. I would rather avoid an awkward scene in any case."

"I knew it!" Lucinda leaped from one foot to the other. "You *do* have an earl and a viscount vying for you!"

"It's not like that at all!" Miranda protested. "I suspect James is being protective, that's all. Why he thinks he has the right, I haven't a clue."

Emily's raised brows suggested she may have an idea, but Miranda refused to speculate.

She wasn't about to alter her course because James wasn't as averse to kissing her as she'd first surmised.

It wasn't like he was ready to hang up his hat and settle into a life of domesticity. Why, the mere mention of marriage had him breaking into a cold sweat.

"And by getting the viscount alone, your aim is to...?" Emily began.

"To have him kiss her, of course!" Lucinda said. "How else will she decide whom to choose?"

Miranda blinked, her sister's assertion running too close to the truth for comfort.

The kissing, not the choosing part, obviously.

Emily, meanwhile, was watching her carefully. "Do you think it's wise to encourage the viscount thusly?"

Since Miranda intended to marry the fellow, she didn't see the problem. "It's not like I am playing him false. You know the colonel intends for us to wed."

"That's not the same as you wanting it though, is it?" Emily countered.

Miranda rubbed at the odd pain to her chest. "I know precisely what I am about. Which is why I need this opportunity to...*oh*, I don't know...get back on track, so to speak. So, will you help me? Please?"

She was prepared to beg if it came to that. But thankfully, Lucinda and Emily agreed to her request without further comment.

They passed under the eaves and entered the house.

Lucinda took Miranda's hand and squeezed. "Don't worry, sis. Everything will work out for the best, you'll see."

Squeezing her hand back, Miranda looked to the ceiling.

If only she could be so sure.

21

Trinkets, Fishes and Wishes

At noon, Miranda joined her sister and friends on the front drive. They were to walk to the village, Alton lying but two miles to the east. The elder matrons had already been taken up in the Dowager Duchess' landau, Lady Whincup one of their number.

A boon for them, Lucinda had giggled as they waved the conveyance on its way.

Seeing no cause for rush, the friends set off at a leisurely pace, taking the occasional short cut through the neighboring squire's fields.

Lucinda and Sarah frequently stopped to pick wildflowers and even managed to persuade Amy to add a few blossoms to her 'hideously plain' bonnet. Which could only attest to the mellowing effects of the country or, perhaps, the unmatched determination of one Lucinda Drayton.

Lucinda approached the village with similar enthusiasm. "*Voilà*," she announced, sweeping her arms out wide. "Welcome to the sleepy hamlet of Alton."

Far from quiet, Alton was a bustling market town that serviced the surrounding landowners and tenants alike.

Walking down High Street, they passed the milliners, the butcher, and Mrs. Brown's Bakehouse. As they approached Hart's Drapery where they'd prearranged to meet up with the rest of their party, they slowed and hesitated by the door.

"No, no, no! I said the *emerald* silk as it will best complement my complexion!" Lady Whincup's shrill voice sliced clean through the storefront.

The friends each looked to the other. Miranda was weighing up whether it was worth suffering the countess for the sake of some cloth when the draper's door swung open to reveal the Dowager Duchess.

"Come along, girls," she said, "you look like a bunch of old ninnies, loitering on the step like that."

Chastised, Miranda hurried in after the others.

Lady Whincup was still haranguing the poor clerk at the counter, so she bypassed the delicate silks and lace at the front of the store and headed for the rows of bombazine hanging on the opposing wall.

Her mother and aunt joined her.

"I see you've discovered where the serviceable fabrics are housed," the Dowager Duchess said wryly. "Right at the back, so you cannot avoid passing the more expensive merchandise first. Hart always was a shrewd fellow."

Lady Nora frowned at the dark bolt of worsted wool Miranda stood beside. "Does anything take your fancy, dear?"

"As I'm after nothing in particular, I thought to purchase a length of ribbon for Rebecca. To compensate for leaving her behind with only our brother for company," she told her.

Her mother smiled. "I doubt our Becca's too distraught, not with her and Jonathan having free rein of the house."

"And the kitchens, don't forget." The Dowager Duchess added. "You're bound to be eaten out of house and home by the time you return, Nora. What with all Becca's baking and Jonathan's obligatory sampling."

Aunt Bethel not only encouraged Rebecca's culinary endeavors but also offered her unfettered access to the manor's kitchens—and Mrs. Potts by extension—whenever she so visited.

Hearing Lucinda's call, they turned to where she stood across the way. Lady Nora waved back in acknowledgement. "I best see what Lucinda requires. I shan't be long."

Considering Lucinda was clutching onto a coil of gold-edged lace as if it were hand-spun by Rumpelstiltskin himself, Miranda doubted her mother would be returning any time soon.

"How are you enjoying the visit so far, my dear?" her aunt asked in the interim. "With all the goings on, we haven't had the chance for a nice coze."

Miranda turned back to her aunt with a smile. "I'm enjoying the visit very much. You know how I adore Rose Manor, and with my friends here too, why, that only adds to my delight."

The Dowager Duchess beamed. "I'm so glad, dear. And what of James? You seemed as surprised as I was when he decided to accept my invitation this year. Yet, ever since his arrival, he's been keeping mostly to himself, which I find rather disconcerting."

Miranda wasn't convinced she was the best person to comment, but said, "Mayhap he's merely finding his feet after being absent for so long."

Her aunt's expression turned thoughtful. "I believe you may have the right of it. A period of adjustment can only be expected. I'm just happy James has finally returned to us. Which reminds me, there's something I wish to discuss with you. Oh, it's nothing untoward," she quickly put in when Miranda frowned. "I've only decided to name James as my chief heir and beneficiary, so Rose Manor and all she encompasses shall be his one day."

Miranda was stunned. "But I thought—"

"That the manor formed part of the duchy?" The Dowager Duchess nodded. "A fair assumption, but I can tell you it's not the case. When it became clear my dear Henry would pass without issue, he purchased Rose Manor so I would have a place to call my own. It was most thoughtful of him."

Miranda reached over to squeeze her aunt's hand. From the little she recalled, her late uncle had possessed a heart of gold.

The Dowager Duchess blinked before continuing. "I wasn't about to bequeath such a gift to just anyone. So, after considerable soul-searching, I decided James was the ideal candidate. The lad's as close to me as any son could be and heaven knows he could do with a proper home. Stanton House holds nothing but unpleasant memories, and that rambling estate of his in Kent? Hardly any memories at all seeing James' father couldn't face returning after poor Margaret's death." She shook her head. "I did manage to corner James long enough once to challenge him on his continued neglect of his ancestral home. But he only laughed, telling me, 'That's why God created land stewards, Godmama!' What that boy needs is a firm guiding hand. A wife to show him what it's like to be part of a real family."

Miranda didn't know what to say.

As for James being master of Rose Manor someday, he could hardly look after his own estates by her aunt's own admission, so she couldn't help but question the wisdom of adding to his responsibilities.

Then there was the question of why her aunt was suddenly telling her this. "You are certainly being generous when it comes to James, but tell me, Aunt. You aren't...ailing, are you?"

The Dowager Duchess laughed. "No, not at all! I'm as fit as a fiddle, never you mind. But one cannot reach my age without considering such matters."

Miranda gave in to the impulse and wrapped her aunt in a tight hug.

"Off with you now," her aunt said. "Find something nice to treat yourself with, and for heaven's sake, do try to enjoy yourself. Life's too short to squander away wallowing in misery and regret."

Miranda hardly thought she was as far gone as that, but she trotted off at her aunt's bidding all the same.

***

After a visit to the milliners—where Lady Whincup declared all the bonnets on display to be hideously provincial—then a stop at the stationer—who had the affront to be clean out of olive-hued parchment—Miranda was in need of refreshment by the time they entered Alton's quaint tea shop.

"Let's sit by the window," Lucinda said, indicating a table on the farthest side of the room.

They moved in that direction as another of Lady Whincup's laughs pierced the air.

"I swear that woman could take an ear off an elephant without even trying," Emily muttered, taking the seat beside Miranda.

Lucinda sat with a snort. "If only Lady Whincup was that talented! I'd happily offer up both my ears rather than suffer another word. Why our aunt chose to invite her truly confounds me."

Amy started to cough, so Emily passed her a napkin.

Meg approached and came to stand by Lucinda's shoulder. "Lord Whincup was a close friend of the late duke, and your aunt could hardly exclude the countess from the invite, could she?"

Lucinda had the grace to blush at the mild reproach.

"In any case," Meg continued with a smile, "you and your suffering ears will be relieved to hear that we've summoned the carriage. Lady Nora has a slight headache and wishes to return to manor."

Miranda went to rise, but Meg laid a hand on her shoulder. "There's no cause for alarm, dearest. Your mother assures us that it isn't a bad attack. Stay and enjoy your tea. We'll see you all back at the manor."

It wasn't long after that Miranda and her friends started back for home. On the way, Lucinda, Annabel, and Sarah took turns speculating which gentlemen they thought would secure the biggest catch of the season, whilst Emily and Amy discussed Maria Edgeworth's latest short story.

Miranda trailed behind.

How easily she could imagine James lording over Rose Manor one day. Seated behind the massive oak desk in the study, pouring over the estate ledgers. Or sipping brandy in the library while catching up on the latest *on dits* from Town. Then, long after last light, carrying his lone candlestick up the marble staircase to his rooms for the night.

That she knew the manor so intimately only made her imaginings the more real.

But as Rose Manor came into view, so did a flood of more disturbing images.

Ones of James teasing his future wife over a cinnamon scroll in the morning room. Or taking turns of the rose garden with said paragon on his arm, only to steal a kiss or two beneath the rose arbor.

Miranda staggered at the sudden pinch to her chest.

Even though James wasn't the marrying type, she certainly had no trouble conjuring him up a bride from mid-air.

"*Do* hurry, Mira," Lucinda called from up ahead. "At this rate we'll miss Aunt Bethel's picnic entirely. I don't know about you, but I'm positively famished after all this exercise."

Miranda sighed and hastened to follow.

She reached the hilltop just as the men were clambering up the other side from the direction of the trout stream.

James, Lord Camden, and Kit led the charge, with the viscount and Lord Dunston a few footfalls behind.

Miranda did her best not to notice how ruggedly windswept James looked. Nor stare at his bare neck, his cravat nowhere to be found.

With a little shake to her head, she turned to Kit, who was marching towards them with his catch outstretched like a badge of honor. "Success!" he declared, smiling widely at them.

James stopped by the solicitor's side and scoffed. "You only won the catch of the day, Burton, because we wagered on numbers not weight."

Miranda looked to Kit's haul, and she had to admit his fish were on the smallish side.

Kit didn't seem bothered by the distinction, however. "Rules are rules, and to contest them now would only scream of poor sportsmanship, wouldn't you agree?"

James harrumphed, but the glimmer in his eyes suggested he was only putting on a show for their benefit.

When he found Miranda's gaze, she quickly turned to Lord Camden, the baron sounding quite put out. "At least neither of you were dealt the dud bait."

James shook his head. "We all had the same bait, you dolt."

"You weren't supposed to mention that in front of the ladies," Lord Camden stage whispered from the corner of his mouth, then smiled to hear the ladies' giggles in response.

Lord Hawthorne and Lord Dunston arrived next, the latter looking baffled. "What has everyone so diverted?"

"Only Lord Frederick here not gracefully accepting defeat as per usual." James smirked as Lord Camden shot him a murderous look.

Relieved to see the viscount, Miranda took a step toward him. "And how did you fair, Lord Hawthorne?"

"I must admit Dunston and I became so caught up in our conversation, we paid scant attention to the fishing. Still, we didn't come away empty-handed, bagging six trout between us."

Miranda obligingly admired his catch.

If it weren't for the fish, one would think the viscount had been taking tea in the parlor, not traipsing over the countryside. Just her luck that his flawless appearance didn't affect her nearly as much as James' rumpled one, which only brought to mind lush meadows, sweet-smelling grass, and kisses...

No, not kisses, *fishes*. Like the ones James was holding up as he addressed his cohort cheerily. "Well gentlemen, we best head to the kitchens and off-load our spoils. I doubt the dear duchess would appreciate us turning up for tea reeking of *eau de piscine*. Excuse us, ladies," he said, leading the troop back to the manor.

Lord Hawthorne held back. "Have our fathers returned?" he asked Miranda.

In lieu of fishing, Earl Sommerville, Lord Whincup, and the colonel had decided to pay the neighboring squire their respects, Sir Marcus having inherited the vast estate after the recent passing of his father.

The extensive whiskey collection he'd received as part of his late father's largesse had little bearing on the decision, Miranda didn't doubt.

"I'm not sure as we've only returned to the manor ourselves," she said. "They're bound to surface in time for tea, though."

"I was hoping to catch them before then," he returned with a frown.

Considering his serious mien, Miranda wondered if he was finally ready to approach her father, and she went both hot and cold at the thought. "It's nothing urgent, I trust?"

"No, nothing that cannot wait," Lord Hawthorne assured her with a smile. He looked down at his trout and grimaced. "Well, I best rid myself of these so I can meet you back at the lake. Until then, Miss Drayton."

Miranda returned his bow with a nod and watched his retreating back.

Why did this courting business have to be so fraught with uncertainty? Life would be much simpler if everyone stated their intentions from the onset, thereby saving all those involved considerable time and energy.

She only wished to be settled. Was that too much to ask?

22

Making a Splash

S tanding back from the crowd, James perused the banquet his godmother had organized for their feasting pleasure.

As per the Dowager Duchess' express specifications, three long trestles had been erected beneath the overshadowing elms, each loaded with an assortment of delicacies. Crabmeat and cucumber sandwiches, little mincemeat pies, and individually iced cakes. All that on the first table alone.

James wasn't remotely tempted by the offerings, though. Not even the quickly dwindling mound of cinnamon scrolls his friend currently stood guard over.

He had to smile as Freddy offered up a scroll in toast, his friend's disgruntlement over the morning's fishing competition seemingly forgotten by his second—no, make that, his third—spiced bun.

James' smile dipped as his gaze found Miranda. Not that he wasn't pleased to see her. She looked especially fine, dressed in some green, gauzy confection that made her eyes shine.

No, his frown was wholly reserved for the viscount, who'd anchored himself to Miranda's left side as if she were his lifeline.

His gaze narrowed even further to see Miranda lay a hand on Hawthorne's arm and angle her head as she smiled up at him.

Whatever could she be about? Miranda wasn't the type to stoop to practiced flirtation. She had no such need, being perfectly enticing just as she was. And when she giggled at something Hawthorne said, the sound rang false to James' ears.

At least in all *their* interactions, Miranda's reactions had been refreshingly instinctive and real. The insight didn't ameliorate his dark mood one bit, however, but he knew what would.

He took a step in Miranda's direction and stopped when his godmother suddenly came upon him.

"James, my boy! What on earth are you doing skulking here in the shadows? I would have thought Lady Whincup, at least, would have caught you by now."

He winced. "Please refrain from mentioning that name to me, Godmother. Whilst the countess may well be your friend, she's naught but a nuisance."

At least he'd managed to avoid the woman thus far. Lady Whincup had Christopher Burton cornered by the punch bowl.

James only hoped the solicitor would keep her occupied for a while. A long, long while...

"Well, there may be extenuating circumstances which go a long way to explaining her behavior," the Dowager Duchess said, "but that's neither here nor there. Besides, her brother is entirely eligible, and I needed him to make up the numbers."

"Dunston? Eligible?" James snorted. "I'm surprised he could drag himself away from his stables long enough to pen an acceptance, let alone attend your house party. He must be languishing from the separation even as we speak."

His comment only seemed to amuse his godmother. "Preoccupation with one's horseflesh is hardly uncommon, dear son. Besides, if I started excluding men on that basis, there'd be scant left to invite."

"True," James acknowledged wryly.

"'Tis *you* that has me concerned, however." The Dowager Duchess raised her eyebrows. "How in heaven's name do you expect to make any ground with my niece from all the way over here? Proximity breeds familiarity you know."

James' jaw clenched.

If his godmother knew just how hell-bent he was on *proximity*, then she'd have realized the issue was a moot point.

Unfortunately, Miranda wasn't so keen on his company, which wasn't surprising given her poor opinion of him.

He'd obviously been too zealous in cultivating his ne'er-do-well reputation.

His stepmother always said it would be his downfall one day. James just never imagined the high price he might have to pay.

Of course, he could hardly share any of this with his godmother. So he said, "It's not as simple as all that. Not with Hawthorne firmly attached to Miranda's hip."

"Pfft, excuses," his godmother dismissed with a wave. "And it's called *courting* in case you'd care to give it a try. Surely, you're not going to stand back and let the viscount steal the march on you?"

James huffed. "Hawthorne's been dancing to Miranda's tune long before I returned on the scene."

"And whose fault is that?" The Dowager Duchess certainly pulled no punches when it came to telling it like it was. "We've already established that you're late to the race, which only makes time more of the essence. Get to it, James, before she's snatched up from beneath your very eyes. A little groveling wouldn't go astray either."

He smarted at that. "You needn't state the obvious, Godmother. In fact, I was on my way over before you detained me for this delightful *tête-à-tête*."

The Dowager Duchess sniffed. "I wouldn't have to spell anything out if you were making any inroads on your own." She made a shooing motion. "Go on then. As I said—"

"Time is of the essence, yes, yes," James echoed sardonically. He didn't get very far, though, what with Lucinda and Miss Burton appearing to block his path.

Seriously, was everyone conspiring to keep him and Miranda apart?

"Ladies, how may I be of assistance?" he asked.

"Oh, we're in no need of help, Lord Stanton," Lucinda stated breezily. "We couldn't bear to see you all alone and thought to offer our company. Isn't that so, Emily?"

Miss Burton nodded as Lucinda launched into speech.

"How did you find the fishing?" she said before going on to answer her own question. "Yes, I recall now. We saw you earlier and it was clear you had a fine time of it, even if Emily's brother managed to trump you at the end. Although personally," she added, lowering her voice, "I agree yours looked to be the far finer catch."

Seeing her finally pause for breath, James opened his mouth. But instead of allowing him to respond, she launched into an account of their visit to Alton with such detail, James could've sworn he'd been right there shopping alongside them. And he may well have been if he hadn't needed the time to process Miranda's startling revelation.

How could her recollection of *that* night be so different from his own?

He flicked a glance to Miranda, only to find she was stealing off into the bushes with Hawthorne.

Resisting the temptation to growl, he said, "If you ladies would excuse me for a moment..." But as he made a move around them, he found himself caught.

Looking down, he glared at Lucinda's fingers that had tightened around his wrist like a manacle. Then over at Miss Burton, who had conveniently become entranced by the bucolic surroundings.

It seemed he wasn't going anywhere soon.

Miranda steered the viscount down the graveled path that led to the grotto, silently congratulating herself on a job well executed.

She'd managed to avoid James—she would thank Emily and Lucinda for their timely interception later—and persuaded Lord Hawthorne to accompany her to her favorite childhood haunt.

Seeing the viscount glare at the undergrowth, she went to reassure him. "It's not much farther, my lord. Though I must admit it's been years since I've ventured this way."

Lord Hawthorne continued to frown. "This all looks terribly overgrown, Miss Drayton. Mayhap we should turn back. We wouldn't wish to become disorientated and lose our way."

Miranda smiled. "There's no chance of that, my lord. My aunt's estate is hardly that vast. Besides, I practically grew up here, so I know these grounds as well as the back of my hand."

Fortunately, the viscount couldn't see the fingers she had crossed in said hand.

"Here it is!" she exclaimed when they finally came upon the grotto.

She tugged on the viscount's sleeve as the path opened up to reveal a majestic spring-fed pool hidden amongst the trees.

"My siblings and I used to play here as children," she recalled in a reverent tone. "Where we imagined a secret world of faeries and water sprites, my brother always playing the bad-tempered ogre."

She chuckled, then quietened to see the viscount's uneasy expression. "Did you and your sisters play similar games in your youth?"

"There was little time for games, Miss Drayton, at least in my case. My days were consumed with my studies, learning the ins and outs of the estate. Then I was off to Eton when of age, of course."

Miranda felt a tinge of sadness at the picture he painted.

Despite being raised under the colonel's tight command, she and her siblings still found time for merrymaking, although accomplishing the feat often required a master in stealth.

But even her father's expectation that she married well paled in comparison to having the duties of an earldom thrust upon one from the cradle.

Miranda turned and squeezed his arm gently. "May I say, I find that a shame, my lord. For we are children but once, and at what other time are we free to act with such abandon?"

The viscount looked surprised. "Whilst your sentiments are certainly appreciated, they are entirely misplaced. I merely took on my duties as anyone in my position would. As indeed, should."

Before Miranda could respond, a loud shriek followed by a tremendous splash had them hurrying back down the path, where they came upon a farcical scene.

Lucinda—looking akin to a drowned rat—was clutched in James' arms after clearly having been pulled from the lake.

Lady Nora was fluttering around them, tutting as she went, whilst the Dowager Duchess stood to the side, barking orders at a wide-eyed footman. The colonel watched on with a frown, and looking to the other guests, their reactions ranged from shock to unbridled delight.

Miranda crossed the clearing and approached the bedraggled pair. "Are you well?" she directed at her sister. "Whatever has happened?"

James looked down to Lucinda, then back at Miranda reproachingly.

Lady Nora stepped in. "Never mind that, Miranda. We need to get your sister back to the house before she catches her death."

James spurned into action. "Allow me," he said, setting a path through the parting crowd, ignoring Lucinda's feeble protests that she was perfectly capable of walking.

Miranda followed, Emily and Kit catching her on the rise.

"I cannot believe my sister allowed this to happen!" she hissed to the pair.

"I doubt it was intentional," came Emily's even reply.

"Not surprising, though," Kit said. "Your sister is an accident waiting to happen."

"That's a bit harsh, don't you think?" Emily said, turning on her brother. "Lucinda's surely feeling terribly embarrassed as it is, thus your criticism hardly helps matters."

"It may inspire her to be more reticent in future," Kit shot back. "One can hope, anyway."

Miranda ignored them as she hurried into the house and paused in the hallway.

James was scaling the staircase with her sister still cradled in his arms.

"I'll see to Lucinda and let you know how she fares," she said to Emily and Kit.

She joined her mother on the stairs, and they followed James and Lucinda to the family wing.

They reached Lucinda's bedchamber just as James was carefully placing her on the bed. He stepped back and the maids swooped in with the blankets.

James wished Lucinda a speedy recovery before heading back to the door.

On his way out, he leveled Miranda an enigmatic look.

But deciphering his odd mood would have to wait. Lucinda's chattering teeth could be heard from the other side of the room.

Rushing to the bed, Miranda helped her mother peel off Lucinda's drenched clothing and pat her dry.

The maids collected the soiled garments and went to organize a bath.

Seeing her daughter safely encased in a fresh set of blankets, their mother also left the room, promising to return with a restorative tisane.

"What a to-do!" Lucinda said once she and Miranda were alone, her voice muffled by the veritable mountain of fleece piled around her.

Whilst relieved to see her sister had regained some of her color, Miranda's tension hadn't abated much, if any at all. "When I asked you to provide a distraction, Lucinda," she began slowly. "I didn't expect you to jump in the lake."

Lucinda blinked, her cheeks coloring even further. "It's not as if I fell into the lake on *purpose*, Miranda. As if I would intentionally humiliate myself in such a manner! The look on everyone's faces..." Her body shuddered at the recollection. "Why are you so upset, anyway? Did I happen to interrupt an intimate moment with your beloved viscount, perchance?"

To her chagrin, Miranda hadn't given Lord Hawthorne the slightest consideration since the drama had unfolded. "No, not at all, and he's not my viscount."

She left the 'beloved' part well alone.

"Ah, so this is about James. I suspected as much."

Miranda stilled at her sister's smug expression.

"You know, Mira," Lucinda went on innocuously. "I cannot believe I ever thought James old. He certainly carried me all the way to my room as if I weighed scant more than a feather. And quite frankly, his actions this afternoon could be described as nothing short of heroic."

Miranda rolled her eyes. "*Please!* You fell into a pond, Lucinda, not the Atlantic. Our aunt's decrepit butler could've retrieved you with much less fanfare. Besides, you know James isn't the one for you."

The mere prospect of her sister and James made Miranda feel distinctly ill.

"Why ever not?" Lucinda was frightfully calm as she pulled her hands from the blankets and started checking off her fingers one by one. "James is charming, for a start, and ever so witty, so one could never be bored in his company. He's a fair dancer, is more than just pleasing to the eye, and quite clearly, a hero. Why, he's the stuff of fantasies. In fact," she declared with a smirk, "I believe James satisfies even my most stringent future husband criteria."

At some point during the litany, Miranda's jaw had dropped, so she closed her mouth with a snap.

"Whatever could be the matter?" Lucinda asked. "You look as if you were the one to swallow a bucketful of pond-water, not I. You cannot be jealous, surely? You cannot have both the earl and the viscount, you know."

Finally finding her voice, Miranda hotly denied the allegation. "Of course, I realize that, Lucinda. Why, this entire conversation is absurd!"

Lucinda raised her brows as if to say, '*Well you started it.*'

Miranda took several deep breaths and fixed her gaze onto the opposing wall.

Then Lucinda said, "I'm only teasing, you know. I definitely do not see James as a potential husband. Not for myself, in any case."

Miranda nodded without turning.

For whilst she knew her sister spoke the truth, she was still struggling for composure.

Lucinda wasn't quite through, though. "However, if James *is* seeking a bride, he won't remain unattached for long. You need only recall the Cumberland's rout where every debutant swooned at the mere sight of him. And here at the manor, you only have to look at Lady Whincup, who throws herself in his path at every available opportunity."

As if Miranda could ever un-see that. "If he falls for *that*...well, he deserves everything he has coming to him."

"Come now, Mira," Lucinda said. "You were never one to give in so easily. Besides, I doubt James is truly interested in the countess, not when he's clearly smitten with you."

A half-laugh escaped from Miranda's mouth.

How preposterous that was.

"You will seriously consider him though? A match with Lord Hawthorne isn't inevitable, you know. Nor should it be if he's not the man you truly want."

Lucinda was a tenacious little thing, like a bug intent on one's picnic lunch.

Miranda made a non-committal sound in response, seeing no point in rehashing that old argument.

"Furthermore," Lucinda went on as if she might never cease, "I'm sure you will make the right decision in the end. You the most sensible of us and all."

Miranda shook her head, thinking her sister's faith entirely misplaced. But seeing her concern came from a place of love, she leaned over the bed and attempted a hug through the wad of blankets. Realizing the futility of the task, she pulled back and opted for an affectionate pat to her cheek instead.

"I'm truly blessed having you as a sister," she said, "and please forgive me for being such a bore. I am not sure what came over me. But enough of me, it's *you* who's in need of cosseting. How are you feeling?"

Lucinda's color was looking much restored, and thankfully, she didn't appear any worse for the mishap.

"I'm feeling much improved," Lucinda said. "Although it's getting a trifle toasty under here."

Miranda reached over to help loosen the blankets. "You know Mother will insist you stay abed for the evening."

"Oh, I expect nothing less, and what daughter would I be not to honor her wishes? I think I can endure a little fussing, with a warm bath, dinner on a tray and the chance to return to my novel. Purely in deference to Mama's nerves, of course."

"Of course." Miranda rolled her eyes at her sister's shameless grin.

Their mother reentered the room then, ladened with a silver tray.

She bustled over to the bed and placed the tray on the side table. "Here you are, Lucinda dear, my special brew as promised." She decanted a healthy helping of the tisane and handed the cup to Lucinda. "You gave me quite the scare earlier. But all's well now you're back safe with me to look after you."

Miranda exchanged an amused look with Lucinda before leaving her to their mother's tender care.

23

Parlor Games

Seeking to escape her thoughts, Miranda headed downstairs well before the bell was to sound for dinner.

She couldn't shake the image of James mounting the staircase with Lucinda banded to his chest like the hero her sister had painted. The action didn't sit well with his reputation as a shameless profligate who only looked to his own interests, and her head pained from trying to figure out which was the true James. The one she remembered from eons gone by, or the face he presented to the world.

Of course, it didn't help that she couldn't trust her instincts when it came to the man.

Having made her way to the drawing room, she paused at the threshold.

The cause of her turmoil was leaning against the back of a chaise as if he'd not a care in the world.

She moved forward, though she was sorely tempted to run in the opposite direction.

Never had she so appreciated the value of the strategic retreat.

James straightened. "Good evening, Miranda. My, how lovely you look."

She looked down and frowned.

She wasn't wearing anything remarkable. Nothing that scores of debutants were swanning around Town in, in any case.

He chuckled. "Do you take exception to every compliment you receive, I wonder, or merely those from my lips? Because if it's the latter, I can assure you. You steal my very breath, no matter what you could be wearing—or not as the case may be."

"You mustn't say such things, James," she admonished.

"I don't see why I should not. Not when it's the absolute truth."

She shook her head.

His compliments slid too easily from his tongue to be taken seriously.

He moved closer, so she took an evasive step back. But he only said, "Tell me, how does your sister fare?"

"Extraordinarily well, considering," she said, latching onto the subject. "Lucinda's even taken to waxing lyrical about your gallantry to anyone unfortunate to be within hearing distance, if you can credit it."

"Good to know my sessions at Gentleman Jack's haven't been completely in vain, then."

Miranda made a point of rolling her eyes.

Considering his stance, she wouldn't be surprised if he were flexing his muscles beneath all his finery.

Not that she had any intention of testing her theory.

"And you, Mira?" he teased, raising his brows. "Were you equally impressed?"

"For simply being in the right place at the right time? Hardly."

He must have caught her telltale flush because his grin widened. "You know, when we're sparing like this, I cannot help but think—"

A sound in the hallway gave him pause, and for once, Miranda wasn't pleased by the interruption.

She was suddenly desperate to hear what he'd been about to say.

Lady Whincup flounced into the parlor and immediately made a beeline for James.

"My Lord Stanton," she said breathlessly, her amble bosom rising and falling almost hypnotically in tandem.

James obligingly bowed over her heavily bejeweled hand. "Lady Whincup, you look well this evening."

Vexingly, it was no exaggeration. The countess looked nothing short of bedazzling, garbed in an emerald gown which perfectly matched the gems dangling from her earlobes, not to mention the enormous jewel she had cradled between her breasts.

Miranda could only have paled in comparison.

"You are too kind, darling," Lady Whincup drawled in a voice so raspy, Miranda briefly considered dispatching a footman to fetch the poor dear a glass of water.

Instead, she said pointedly, "And Lord Whincup? He's not to join us this evening?"

The countess finally turned to acknowledge her presence. "Miss Drayton, my apologies. I failed to see you there. In answer to your question, poor Whincup is overset from his exertions this afternoon, thus has sensibly elected to take a tray in his room."

The lady didn't look too disheartened by the loss, considering the meaningful side glance she sent James' way.

"Then do pass on our wishes to his lordship for his speedy recovery," Miranda said with a sugary smile.

The atmosphere turned decidedly frosty then, so Miranda was relieved to see Aunt Bethel and Meg enter the room.

She started in their direction, but James anticipated her move, his fingertips grazing the inside of her arm as he took her by the elbow.

"Ah, here is Her Grace and Mrs. Barlow now," he said. "They are undoubtedly awaiting an update on Miss Lucinda. If you would excuse us, Lady Whincup."

"Until later, Lord Stanton," she cooed as James steered Miranda away.

Only such a woman could make such a statement sound equal part threat, part promise.

***

In the parlor later that evening, James was drawn into a game of Buffy Gruffy. He would much rather have partnered

Miranda at the whist table, but Hawthorne had been granted that privilege.

Glancing over to the card players, he caught Miranda's eye, and she quickly returned to her cards with a frown.

A ripple of laughter had him turning back to the group, where Dunston had his finger to his nose as he hopped about on one foot. His forfeiture for incorrectly guessing which of Freddy's sisters had been seated before him.

Lady Whincup moved to take her turn next, so James wisely vacated his seat.

If one needed any guidance on the art of pursuit, he need only look to Lady Whincup's fine example.

He went to the sideboard and poured two glasses of sherry, then headed to where Miranda was seated with Hawthorne, Lord Sommerville and Meg.

"Are you well, Miss Drayton?" the viscount was saying. "As you seem distracted this evening."

Miranda placed down her cards and sighed. "I'm afraid the afternoon's events have finally caught up with me."

"It seems I've brought restoratives at precisely the right moment, then," James said.

Ignoring Hawthorne's scowl, he handed a glass to Meg, then leaned closer to Miranda and passed her the other.

"Contemplating a lifetime of dreary evenings with only Hawthorne for company," he said so only she could hear. "That would be cause enough for anyone to sigh."

Miranda sucked in a breath. "At least I'd have the comfort of having my husband home every night."

"Honestly, is that how you envisage your future? Surely you want more from life than that."

She looked to Hawthorne. But seeing Meg had engaged him in conversation, she turned back with a hiss. "Why, are you offering yourself as a viable alternative?"

James smiled.

If her aim was to shock, she'd misfired completely.

"If I were so lucky and you did happen to choose me, then be assured, I would keep you happily entertained *all* night long, where any sighs you made wouldn't be ones of boredom."

Miranda blushed, her mouth opening, though no words escaped.

Hawthorne shot him a disgruntled lock from across the table, which James took as his cue to retreat—for the interim.

He went to pour himself a drink. But hearing Miranda make her excuses to Hawthorne, he abandoned the sideboard and met her halfway across the room.

"A moment of your time, Miranda, if I may?"

"No, you may not," she retorted, looking mighty pleased with herself as she glided straight past him.

Despite his annoyance, he had to admit to being more than a little roused by her showing of fortitude. In more ways than one.

"I thought you might appreciate some fortification," Freddy said, coming to stand by his side.

James tore his gaze from Miranda's retreating silhouette and took the proffered glass of claret. He took a deep swallow and met his friend's gaze over the rim.

"Things not going to plan, I take it?" Freddy said.

James snorted at the understatement and flicked a glance to the now-empty doorway.

If he were a lessor man, he might wallow at the loss.

Fortunately, he came from a long line of Stantons who consisted of sterner stuff.

"Fancy a game of billiards?" he directed at his friend, setting off to the hallway without awaiting a response.

James had the table set up by the time Freddy sauntered into the billiard room.

Freddy handed him a cue and waved for James to proceed him. "So what's your next move? Roses on the lady's pillow? Serenades by moonlight? A wayward arrow to her beloved beau's heart in tomorrow's archery tournament?"

James broke with satisfactory force, then sank the red ball in the far-right pocket. "Yes, to all the above."

Freddy grinned as he went to take his turn. "So it's game on then."

James tipped his cue.

He couldn't have put it better himself.

***

With their guests finally abed, Bethel and Meg settled down in the library, savoring the quiet along with their glasses of port.

Bethel sighed in satisfaction. "The house party's progressing well, wouldn't you agree, my dear? With all the guests rubbing along famously, although Lady Whincup a mite too famously, mayhap. But overall, I believe this may prove to be our best party yet. And what more could we fine hostesses ask for, I say."

Meg smiled back, her gray eyes soft in the firelight. "For the most part, dear heart, I concur. Although it must be said, some are getting along better than others."

Bethel shook her head. "So tell me, what has my numskull of a godson gone and done this time?"

She listened as Meg outlined the terse exchange between Miranda and James that she'd overheard at the whist table earlier that evening.

"Whatever could be wrong with that boy?" Bethel made an exasperated sound. "James is being frightfully obtuse, and after all my well-meaning advice too. I told him to *court* Miranda, not aggravate her. Hardly surprising then if she withdraws from him even further. But admittedly, my niece isn't faring much better when it comes to the romance stakes."

Meg's lips twisted wryly. "Miranda's not exactly receptive to our lad's advances, is she? However sore they may be."

Bethel snorted. "Not that one can blame her, considering. Still, I've tried doing my part, dangling the possibility of a future at Rose Manor right under her nose. But I fear that too has come to naught. Miranda is as obstinate as her father when it comes to something she's already set her mind upon!"

Meg frowned. "But I thought you'd already willed the house to Miranda, so how does it play into this?"

"I may have suggested that I intended for James to inherit. Nothing like an added incentive to hasten things along."

"You are a wicked woman, Your Grace."

Bethel raised her glass. "I see nothing for it, my love, but to continue throwing Miranda and James together with the hope they'll communally grow some sense. Failing that, I have not ruled out knocking their heads together. Repeatedly, if necessary. For it seems obvious to everyone bar themselves that they are made for each other."

"You think it will work though, Bea?"

"It must. It certainly couldn't make matters any worse!" Bethel declared, finishing her port in one swallow. "Besides, despite all the excitement, I fear we're getting too old for this nonsense."

"Speak for yourself," Meg said, rising to her feet. "Personally, I'm feeling quite restored after our nightcap. In fact, I wager I could beat you up to our suite."

"Right!" Bethel accepted the challenge with relish. "I may have a couple of years on you yet, missy, but you've forgotten the sheer magnitude of the Drayton determination."

And with much pushing and shoving, the giggling hostesses made for the stairs.

24

Tell Me a Story

Whilst Miranda was pleased to see her sister back in fine form the following morning, she was admittedly a little envious. Oh, to be so carefree.

She longed for a simpler time when the hardest decision she had to make was what to have for breakfast. Even then, she almost always reverted to her favored coddled eggs and toast. Mayhap what she was experiencing was something of the same vein: James was just an unfortunate habit that she needed to break.

So when Lucinda suggested the ladies convene in the drawing room for a reading of *Miss M's Mysteries*—the latest edition of *La Belle Assemblée* having been delivered that morning—Miranda had jumped at the opportunity. Her aunt's guests were in for a real treat—her sister having honed her oratory skills from years of devout practice—and Miranda could well do with focusing on someone else's dramas for a while.

She followed the others into the parlor, a quick scan of the room revealing no sign of Lady Whincup. Miranda sent up her reverent thanks for the unexpected reprieve and went to sit on the chaise next to Emily and her brother, Kit, who'd obviously decided to join the spectacle.

She exchanged a smile with the pair, hoping the audience would be kind for Emily's sake.

"Is everyone settled?" Lucinda asked once everyone had taken a seat.

At their nods, she opened the periodical and cleared her throat. Just as she was about to begin, Lord Camden skidded to a stop in the doorway.

"Whoa!" Freddy's eyes widened. "I haven't stumbled upon a secret women's meeting of some sort, have I?"

He looked positively green at the prospect.

Lucinda sniffed. "Clearly not, Lord Camden. We would hardly choose to convene in such a public arena if that were indeed the case. Besides," she added, flicking a meaningful glance at Kit, "Mr. Burton is here."

"I see, my mistake," Freddy muttered, appearing no less confounded.

Lucinda waved him in. "You may as well join us, my lord."

"Yes, do," the Dowager Duchess seconded from her place by Lucinda. "Another male perspective certainly wouldn't go astray."

"Well, if nothing else, I can provide that," Freddy said, flashing a grin.

As Lord Camden went to sit by his sisters, Miranda leaned closer to Emily. "My, isn't *Miss M* popular this morning?"

Emily blushed, looking eminently pleased.

And why shouldn't she?

Miranda was proud of her friend for all she'd achieved.

With Lord Camden situated, Lucinda was poised to resume.

Then James swaggered into the room.

"For heaven's sake!" Lucinda huffed, eerily echoing Miranda's sentiments. "No one else is hovering in the hall, I take it?"

James shook his head.

"Good! Then if you would kindly take a seat beside Miranda, I will begin."

Miranda tracked his approach from the corner of her eye.

There went her hope for some blessed escapism.

It was a bit difficult to deny someone's very existence when he was sitting right beside you.

James took his seat as duly directed and frowned to see Miranda's posture stiffen.

She hardly looked comfortable pressed against the arm of the chaise like that.

If only he could put her at ease.

He wasn't a threat; he only desired her company. Hence, he'd been quick to the parlor when he heard the ladies had gathered for a reading of some sort.

Lucinda began to speak, her voice almost hypnotic as she started to weave what was clearly shaping up to be quite a farcical tale.

Still his attention remained fixed on Miranda, and he smiled to see her relax as the story unfolded, her expression changing from one of wonder to amusement, then turning ashen when her sister mentioned something about a poor mort being stabbed in a garden.

He leaned closer. "I didn't take you for a squeamish sort."

She turned her head and snorted. "With Jonathan as a brother? Impossible."

His smile widened, and her expression softened. Then the clearing of someone's throat had them turning back to their narrator.

James pretended to listen for a while, but it wasn't long before his gaze drifted back to the paragon seated beside him.

Her cheeks had taken on a rosy glow, and the devil in him veered closer, only to retreat again when she shook her head in silent warning.

Desperate for any connection, however slight, he looked to the hand she had set on the cushions between them and traced the elegant lines of her fingers with his gaze. Reaching across, he rested his hand just to the left of hers.

If he inched but a little her way, their pinkies would touch.

"And what says you, Lord Stanton?" Lucinda suddenly addressed him.

Looking up, his cheeks heated to find the numerous sets of eyes pinned on him.

Only then did he realize that not only had the reading concluded, but he was also expected to contribute to the post-reading discussion.

Too bad he hadn't been attending, thus had no opinion whatsoever.

"Do you think *Miss M's* discovery will be the key to unmasking the murderess?" Lucinda pressed.

"Perhaps," he said, thinking to brazen it out.

Then, quite unexpectedly, Miranda came to his aid. "That would depend on whether the snagged piece of velvet could be tied to The Scarlet Lady at all, wouldn't it? If the culprit were truly clever, she would dispose of the cloak upon discovering the tear."

There were several titters of agreement before the conversation turned to the possible identity of this so-called Scarlet Lady. Then the tea service arrived, and the room's attention diverted to the steaming plate of cinnamon scrolls the Dowager Duchess' housekeeper went to reveal with great fanfare.

James turned to Miranda in the ensuing melee. "Thanks for rescuing me back there."

She eyed him askance. "For saving you from Lucinda's wrath when it became clear you hadn't been attending, you mean?" At his bashful nod, she added, "Make no further mention of it. Although how you could've missed even a second of my sister's performance remains a mystery even *Miss M* would be at pains to solve."

"That's hardly a great a mystery at all, I would think," he said. "Mira—"

She shot to her feet before he could finish, giving him no option but to follow her up.

"I vowed to find Lord Hawthorne after the reading concluded," she blurted, looking wildly to the room as if expecting the man to be lurking somewhere amongst the furniture. "I wouldn't want to keep him waiting."

James bit back a retort.

He would wager his very last farthing that she hadn't thought of her precious viscount until that very moment.

She obviously didn't require a response anyhow as she was already halfway across the room.

Her tendency to flee was becoming a real nuisance. He couldn't tie her down, after all. Still, her skittishness could only mean he was making an impact.

Now to bring the whole godforsaken wall tumbling down.

In the hallway, Miranda paused by the grandfather clock to take in a deep breath. Then she caught sight of her quarry. Not the viscount as she may have suggested to James, but Emily as she was exiting the parlor.

"I need to speak with you. *Privately*," she said, drawing her friend into a nearby anteroom and closing the door.

Emily raised her brows. "Is anything amiss?"

"Is anything amiss?" Miranda repeated flatly. "You might say that. Whatever were you thinking, having Lord Brutus stabbed to death beneath a *rose arbor* of all places!"

"Oh, that." Emily didn't even bat an eyelash. "If I recall correctly, I was thinking of our conversation at the Cumberland Ball and wished to dispense a little poetic justice on your behalf. I may not be able to slay your dragons literally, Mira, but *figuratively*, now that's something I can work with."

"Yes, yes," Miranda said, "I appreciate the sentiment—which is sweet in a convoluted kind of way—but what if James had made the connection?"

Emily laughed. "Well, I have to admit I hardly expected Lord Stanton to see the piece, let alone have the whole scene read to him *verbatim*. But no harm was done since it was clear he wasn't even attending. I'm a little insulted actually, now I come to think of it."

Miranda rubbed her neck at a particularly tender spot. "I just cannot help thinking if he ever suspected…"

Emily looked at her curiously. "That you stumbled upon him and his mistress in the garden that Christmas? Even if he did—which would be highly unlikely at this late a date—tell me, would it really matter?"

"Of course, it *matters*," Miranda said incredulously. "James thinks I kissed him that night because I was bosky. So if he ever discovered that I caught him cozying up to Lady Edwina the next day, and the sight overset me so much I went and blabbed to my best friend all about it, he would realize…" She stopped short, snapping her mouth shut.

"Yes," Emily pressed. "He would realize…"

"Nothing," Miranda said, clenching her jaw. "Absolutely nothing. You were right in the first instance. It's of no consequence."

Emily frowned. "I'm worried for you, Mira. You haven't been yourself the entire house party. What is it about Lord Stanton that oversets you so much?"

"Oh, Em, I'm just so confused. Before I came here, I had a clear picture of what my future would entail. Now for one reason or another, that vision has been hacked to pieces, and mostly by my own hand."

"Something has happened," Emily concluded shrewdly. "You can tell me, you know. I'd be the last person to judge you."

Miranda shook her head.

As much as she was tempted to lay the whole sorry mess bare, she couldn't. At least, not without losing her composure completely. Besides, Emily couldn't possibly help.

The battle Miranda was waging was mainly within her own mind.

"So, what are you planning to do now?" Emily asked in the fraught silence.

"If only I knew," Miranda replied honestly. "If only I knew."

25

Winners and Losers

By the time the afternoon's amusements on the front lawn came around, Miranda was no closer to a resolution.

She'd intended to spend the rest of the day with Lord Hawthorne after neglecting him all morning, thinking his steadying presence would reassure her that she was on the right path. But as soon as the archery tournament had concluded, Lady Whincup dragged the viscount and James off for lawn bowls, and Miranda would much rather a visit to the tooth drawer than suffer another second of the countess.

Instead, she'd joined her sister and Emily in a 'friendly game of quoits' against Kit, Lord Camden, and Lord Dunston.

"Whatever was that?" Lucinda directed at Miranda, throwing her arms up in disgust. "You overshot the peg by a clear foot! I fear your concentration, if not your eyesight, has completely abandoned you."

Miranda did not dignify her sister's remark with a response.

Lord Camden took his turn next and whooped as another of his rings easily found the peg.

"That makes us nine to seven," Kit declared, tossing one of his rings in the air and deftly catching it in the other. He congratulated Freddy for the fine shot, then turned back to Lucinda with a grin. "Might as well concede defeat, Miss Lucinda, seeing it's virtually impossible for you to win from this point."

"Never!" Lucinda scowled. "Let's make it the best of twelve, shall we?"

Miranda groaned inwardly, realizing her sister wasn't about to relent any time this century.

Kit scoffed. "I hardly think drawing this out will result in a different outcome."

"Fine, *Christopher*," Lucinda said, knowing how much it irritated Kit to be addressed by his given name. "I challenge you to a game of shuttlecock instead. It will be the Drayton Destroyers versus the Burton Battlers!"

"We're descending into clan warfare now, I take it?" Emily said, looking distinctly pained.

A feeling Miranda could well understand as she tried to curb her sister. "I think we're done here, Lucinda. This is bordering on the absurd, don't you think?"

"By way of the road to ridiculous," Kit muttered, the sentiment earning him a glare from both Lucinda and Emily.

"See!" Lucinda gestured wildly in Kit's direction. "We cannot let him win. Just look at him! Yesterday's fishing competition has clearly gone straight to his oversized head."

Miranda took her sister's arm as a precaution.

"Well, I'm famished," Lord Camden declared suddenly, his cheerful voice doing little to dispel the escalating tension. "I think I shall join Ned in the refreshment tent."

Lord Dunston had edged away from their group and was starting up the rise.

Miranda only wished she'd had the foresight to follow him.

"Admit it, Lucinda, you've lost. The Drayton Defeated!" Kit declared.

Miranda tightened her grip on her sister's forearm.

Lucinda looked poised to launch her quoits straight at the unsuspecting lawman's head.

"Come along, Kit." Emily took her brother by the arm, shooting Miranda a sympathetic look as she all but dragged her twin to the rotunda.

Miranda turned to deal with her own sibling.

"You really shouldn't let him rile you so," she said, dropping her sister's arm now the danger had passed. "You have to admit, though, we had a good showing in the archery, the gentlemen only beating us at the last."

In fact, Miranda had struck home twice.

Envisioning James' face at the center had done wonders for her aim.

"It wasn't enough though, was it?" Lucinda grumbled. "I cannot tolerate that pompous, self-important, arrogant a—"

"Fancy a stroll in the gardens, Lu? A chance to clear our heads, so to speak?"

"No, no, you go ahead." Lucinda waved her hand. "After all the disappointment, I find myself in dire need of a cinnamon scroll, or two. And knowing Lord Camden as we do, supplies will be dwindling as we speak."

As Lucinda primed herself for another battle—of the gastronomic variety, this time—Miranda spun on her heel and headed in the opposite direction.

She should have joined her sister in the refreshment tent, but she couldn't face the others yet. James would be there, and heaven knew how her brain turned to mush whenever he was near.

Just look at this morning, when she'd been seated beside him in the parlor. He only had to place his hand on the chaise next to her own and she'd trembled, so great was the temptation to reach out and cover his hand with her own.

His being at the manor brought back too many memories, stirred up too many long-forgotten feelings.

She may as well abandon her avoidance strategy, the little good it did. Her thoughts had a habit of returning to James whether he was nearby or not!

Miranda silently cursed, having unwittingly having come upon the rose arbor. At a rustling sound from within, she edged closer and squinted, not quite believing what her eyes were telling her.

Surely, not again!

But yes, there James was, entangled with yet another red-haired beauty beneath the blooming archway!

Miranda almost laughed at the irony. It was either that or cry.

At least he wasn't kissing her.

Not yet. But it was wretchedly close. Not that she intended to wait around for the inevitable.

She still hadn't recovered from the first time.

Turning abruptly, she made for the manor, calling herself every kind of fool for even entertaining the notion that James might have changed.

She entered the hall and was waylaid by her father's summons from the direction of the library.

She paused to compose herself and took a deep breath before entering the room. "Yes, sir? You wished to speak with me?"

How she managed to conceal inner torment, she would never know.

The colonel regarded her coolly from his position behind the desk. "Tell me my eyes are deceiving me, my girl, and you're not running off to your room yet again?" He removed his spectacles and carefully placed them to the side. "I am truly starting to wonder where your head is at. Now's not the time for wavering, but for action! The groundwork has been laid, and the key players are in position. All that remains is for you to bring them home."

"I'm well aware of that, Father," Miranda said. "I'll do better, I promise. No more distractions."

"See that you do!" The colonel rose from behind the desk and came to stand by her side. He searched her face, and whatever he found was cause enough to sigh. "I only want what's best for you, Miranda. And as Lord Hawthorne is clearly the best of the bunch, he is the one we will have. Thankfully, like me, you do not suffer fools gladly. As such, you cannot fail to appreciate the wisdom of our choice."

Miranda nodded.

She could hardly disagree, could she? Especially after what she'd just witnessed outside.

"Good," her father said. "Now go and do whatever needs doing to regroup and reemerge as the warrior I know you to be."

Miranda made a quick exit. But scaling the staircase, she felt more battle weary than anything.

Reaching her bedchamber, she shut the door with a thud and rubbed at her aching temples.

Her father's recriminations were unnecessary. She was well aware that she'd lost sight of the prize.

By allowing James to worm his way back into her thoughts—and dare she admit it, her affections—she'd forgotten herself.

Shaking off her dejection, she reached for the bell.

If she tucked herself up in bed, she could close her eyes and pretend this was all a dream, and everything would right itself again when she next arose.

Unwilling to wait, she started attacking the fastenings at the back of her gown, grunting in frustration as she grappled with the tiny buttons.

Why did they make the blasted things so difficult to undo?

One wouldn't need to disrobe in a hurry, that was for sure.

It wasn't long before her door opened and closed just as swiftly with a soft click.

"Thank goodness, Abigail," she said, her back to the door. "I'm not feeling well and could do with a lie down. If you could just help with my stays..."

Her request was met with silence.

Ridiculous, she thought with a shake to her head.

Nevertheless, she was mindful to keep a tight hold on her bodice before turning.

"You!"

James was leaning against her door, his chest heaving as if he'd just doubled it up the stairs.

He must have followed her from the garden.

Just marvelous.

"Whatever are you about?" she demanded. "You cannot be discovered here." Her eyes darted to the door. "My maid will arrive at any moment!"

It was only then that James seemed to realize where he stood.

While he came to terms with his location, Miranda frantically adjusted her bodice, stilling the moment he turned back to her.

"If you'd just allow me to explain."

Her eyes widened. "There's no need to explain. Whomever you chose to dally with is not my affair."

"I beg to differ," he said, looking quite put out by her declaration. "Besides, it's not how it appeared."

She snorted.

Did he genuinely believe she was that dimwitted?

"I saw well enough to draw my own conclusions, thank you very much. In any case, now's clearly not the time to discuss it."

She swept out her hand in emphasis, losing the tenuous grip of her bodice.

She grasped at the fabric to preserve what remained of her modesty.

His gaze blazed a slow trail down the length of her body, and Miranda couldn't breathe.

Dear Lord. He really had to go.

"If you are quite finished," she snapped, raising her brows when his gaze finally returned to eye level. "In case you misheard, I asked you to leave. Surely you must realize the consequences if we are found together?"

If the threat of a forced marriage didn't have him running all the way back to London, she didn't know what would.

But instead of quaking in his boots, he smiled and took a step closer. Then they both froze at the sound of approaching footsteps.

"Quick, Abigail's coming," she said. "For heaven's sake, don't just stand there, you dolt. Hide!"

26

The Greatest Temptation

Miranda didn't breathe again until James was safely concealed behind the privacy screen on the other side of the room.

She turned to the door as her maid scurried in.

Abigail stopped abruptly. "Are you well, miss? You look frightfully pale."

Miranda suppressed a manic laugh.

Hiding a man in your bedchamber could do that to a person.

"I'm fine, Abigail," she said. "Just a slight headache, that's all. Nothing a short rest won't remedy."

"Of course, miss." Abigail hurried to her side.

Miranda turned, and the maid made quick work of removing her gown and corset.

When a cool draft brushed her heated skin, Miranda reconsidered the wisdom of allowing Abigail to strip her down to her shift with James still in the room.

Unfortunately, it was too late to alter course.

"I do hope you are not catching a chill, my lady," Abigail said. "As the scullery maids tell it, there's some nasty ague going 'round. How 'bout I ring for a bath? It would warm you nice and proper and ease that tension from your shoulders."

"*No!*" Miranda winced, hearing her sharp tone. Although it did mask the strangled cough coming from the other side of the room. "Thank you, but that won't be necessary. I know you have Mother and Lucinda to attend to before dinner," she continued more evenly.

She followed her maid to the bed and climbed inside.

Abigail tucked the bedclothes around her. "If you are quite certain, miss. If not a bath, a cold compress, perhaps? You do look rather flushed."

Miranda closed her eyes. "Honestly, I'll be fine. There's no need to fuss."

Abigail was a dear, but truly, this wasn't the time.

"I will leave you, then." Abigail finally stepped back. "I'll return in an hour to dress you for dinner. If you are feeling up to it, that is."

"Thank you," Miranda said with no little relief, her breath whooshing out as the door closed on the maid.

She hitched the coverlet up to her chin and eyed the privacy screen warily.

Right on cue, James stepped from behind the screen, and she could do little but stare as the incredibility of the situation suddenly hit her.

James Edward Charles Stanton was in her bedchamber!

No good could come of it. None whatsoever.

Her eyes narrowed as he grinned.

"That certainly proved thrilling," he said.

The bounder calmly walked to her writing desk, swiped the chair from underneath and carried it to the bedside, then calmly seated himself as if settling in for a long coze.

Well, that wouldn't do at all.

"Comfortable?" she all but seethed.

His lips twitched. "Quite. Thanks for the asking."

"Oh, don't thank me," she said. "Please remove yourself from my bedchamber and be sure to close the door on your way out, because you are certainly not welcome here. Not now, *not ever.*"

She didn't know how to express herself any clearer.

He shrugged off her words like a piece of lint from his sleeve. "Whyever the rush, Mira? As your maid so kindly informed us, we have plenty of time within which to continue our discussion before she returns."

Miranda bristled, recalling exactly what had prompted their *discussion* in the first place.

A fresh wave of anger—and yes, hurt—hit her full force.

There had to be some way to expunge James from her room, short of throwing something at his insolent head. Although the candlestick at her bedside was practically leaping at the opportunity...

As Miranda continued to scowl at him, James contemplated how best to correct her misapprehension.

He certainly understood how bad things seemed.

Had he realized Lady Whincup's idea of gratitude came in the form of a mauling, he would never have agreed to escort the women back to the house. And now he feared the unfortunate episode had cost him the precious ground with Miranda he'd so painfully regained.

He could only curse for not detangling himself sooner.

What he didn't regret was his current situation. This despite the near agony of seeing Miranda trussed up in her virginal bedclothes like some Christmas gift begging to be unwrapped.

She was temptation personified, and it was all he could do to stay rooted to the chair when all he wanted was nearer. Much nearer. Right in the bed with her, in fact.

He gripped his fingers together and tramped down his baser urges.

He needed to earn Miranda's forgiveness, otherwise he'd never win back her trust.

If he'd ever had her trust in the first place.

"As I was trying to explain before your maid interrupted, what you saw in the garden wasn't what you think. Lady Whincup caught me unexpectedly. I certainly wasn't seeking her attentions, and if you'd only waited but a moment longer, you would have seen me cast her aside. I would *never* dally with another's wife."

Miranda considered him for the longest moment, and whilst she didn't look entirely convinced, she nodded. "Fine, I believe you. In this instance, anyway. Let's leave it at that, shall we? Now you've gotten want you wanted, would you please go?"

She looked pointedly to the door.

"Whilst I'm heartened to hear you believe me, Miranda," he said gravely, "you find me nowhere near satisfied."

And that's when he acted.

Miranda blinked.

One moment, James was seated by her bedside, conversing with her from a relatively safe distance away. Then in the next, he was on her bed with one hand pressed to her cheek and the other gently prying her fingers from the counterpane so to interlace their hands.

She looked at their entwined fingers in a daze.

She couldn't remember the last time they'd touched without the benefit of gloves, and her palm tingled to feel his bare skin pressed against hers.

Frowning, she went to snatch her hand away but made the mistake of looking up.

James was so close, she could almost feel the heat blazing from the golden flecks of his eyes.

"Mira," he breathed. "Surely you've realized by now. You're the only one I desperately want to kiss. May I?"

Miranda nodded, surprised he would even think to ask.

Kissing him seemed as inevitable as June following May.

He dipped his head, and she shuddered the moment their lips met.

Her hands crept to his shoulders as his mouth danced against hers. Stroking, teasing, *tantalizing*. Then he withdrew ever so slightly, and she had to chase his lips else the moment might end.

He brought his fingers to her hair, anchoring her in place.

Overcome with sensation, her whole body came alive, pulsating from his touch. His right hand drifted, tracing the long length of her neck, brushing her shoulder before continuing on its downward path until it came to rest against her breast. She whimpered as his thumb found her nipple and stroked, repeating the motion until the peak came to a sharp point, his mouth moving to her neck, plying her with soft kisses all the while.

"The things you do to me, sweetheart," he rasped by her ear.

With those words, the spell was broken. For Miranda knew she never was, nor would ever be, his 'sweetheart'.

She pushed at his chest, angry at herself for allowing this to happen.

Hadn't she vowed never to kiss him again?

"I'm not one of your flirts, James, and I refuse to be treated as such!"

Rearing back, he leaped off the bed. "How could you say let alone think such a thing? I would *never* take you for a woman of easy virtue."

Miranda's lips twisted bitterly as she looked away.

Of course, he wouldn't. She was nothing like the showy, buxom...*ladies* he so preferred.

"I want you to go. Please, just go."

She no longer cared if she sounded desperate, so long as he let her be.

James rocked back on to his heels, his mind reeling.

With Miranda's ebony tresses all tussled and her lips ripe from their kisses, he was having trouble keeping his thoughts in line.

He stifled a groan.

Get ahold of yourself, man!

It wasn't as if he'd never seen a well-kissed woman before. Whilst nowhere near the libertine the gossips painted him, he wasn't a monk.

Still, he wasn't fooling anyone with such talk, let alone himself.

This wasn't any odd woman, but *Miranda*. The woman he not only loved but wanted with such intensity, he doubted even a pack of rabid wolves could tear him from her side.

Without thinking, he made a move back towards the bed.

Miranda gasped and pulled the sheet to better cover herself. "For heaven's sake, James, get out!"

Wonderful. Now she looked absolutely terrified.

James pulled at his hair and mumbled a curse beneath his breath.

He knew she had the right of it. He had to leave as he couldn't trust himself not to clamber back onto the bed and finish what they'd started.

But before he went, he'd make it clear exactly what she meant to him.

"I am sorry, Mira. I did not intend for things to get quite so out of hand."

"The only apology I wish to hear is the sound of that door closing behind you," she said tersely. "This is the last time I will say it, James. Get. Out. Of. My. Room!"

Poised to argue, he closed his mouth at the sound of movement in the hall. He couldn't have them discovered.

As much as he wanted Miranda, he didn't want her by default.

He wanted her to choose him of her own free will.

With that in the forefront of his mind, he backed away.

He *would* fix this, somehow. Once they both had the chance to calm down and he could be assured that they wouldn't be disturbed.

When he reached the door, he paused, his hand on the doorknob. "I am leaving but this discussion isn't over, Miranda. Not by a long shot."

He opened the door a crack and peered outside, ensuring the hallway was clear before exiting the room, even though leaving her went against all his instincts.

He paused, the door to Miranda's bedchamber pressed against his back.

As much as his insides were screaming to turn right back around, he decided to heed to prudence for once and set off toward his own chamber instead.

Miranda had called his bluff, and rightly so. Now his only recourse was to follow through.

27

The Challenge

In his godmother's parlor later that evening, James was feeling a little tetchy.

Miranda had studiously avoided all eye contact throughout dinner, barely exchanging two words with him.

It was as if everything that had happened upstairs earlier that day had been naught but a pleasant daydream.

Some reticence on her part, he could well understand. But to act as if nothing had changed, and worse, still be encouraging that fool viscount, well, that left James at a complete loss.

So much for laying all his cards on the table.

Instead, he found himself looming at the outer edge of the drawing room, making polite conversation with people he had no desire whatsoever to converse with, and striving to look as if he wasn't on the verge of marching straight over to Miranda and demanding an explanation.

And as if that wasn't enough to contend with, Lady Whincup was heading his way.

"It pains me to see you looking so forlorn, Lord Stanton," she said, brushing his arm as she slithered around to face him. "Why don't we find a cozy corner where you can unburden yourself? You'll feel much better after sharing your troubles, I'm sure."

Quite happy with his solitary musings, James didn't appreciate her intrusion. Nor was he in the mood to be polite about it either. "For the last time, Patricia, leave off. I am not interested."

"That's not the impression you gave me earlier."

He raised a brow.

The countess was clearly delusional as well as relentless.

"Then you are under a misapprehension, I'm afraid. My interest lies elsewhere."

Her expression turned ugly. "And they say women like to blow hot and cold, but you, sir, take the cake." She flicked a malicious glance toward Miranda. "She won't have you, you know."

"I'm not sure I comprehend your meaning, madam."

"Then you are a fool to think you stand a chance. It's clear the lady prefers Lord Hawthorne. Sometimes there's just no accounting for taste, hmm?"

James moved closer. "You will not speak of Miss Drayton to me again, my lady, or indeed to anyone. Do I make myself clear?"

The countess whipped her head back and narrowed her eyes. "As crystal, my lord."

"Good."

He went to the sideboard and poured himself a generous measure of brandy. He threw it back in one swallow before pouring another and turning back to the room.

His gaze immediately found Miranda, who was now nestled on the sofa with Miss Burton.

Freddy trundled over. "Mind if I join you?"

James shrugged.

His friend could demmed well do what he liked. It wasn't like James was his keeper.

Freddy poured himself a drink. "Come now, old chum. It cannot be as grim as all that."

James turned to face him, and Freddy stepped back.

"Right-e-o. I'll leave you to it, then," Freddy said, taking off with his drink. In search of more congenial company, most probably.

James returned to his brooding.

Miranda looked up and shot him an aggravated glare, and he smiled back humorlessly. Then the viscount stepped into his line of vision, blocking Miranda from view.

A misdemeanor in itself.

"Hawthorne," he glowered.

"Stanton." The viscount's response was equally frosty.

James poured himself another drink.

Hawthorne wasn't a complete dunderhead. He would get the hint and leave. Eventually.

"I know what you are about," Hawthorne said, his voice as stilted as his stance, "and I won't stand for it."

Turning back, James lifted his brows. "Indeed?"

"Yes, *indeed*. Hence, I propose we resolve this as gentlemen. A fencing match to prove our mettle. What say you?"

James' lips curled up in surprise. "Challenge accepted. Rapiers or sabers?"

"Sabers." The viscount was quick to put forward.

"Excellent." James' smile turned deadly. "I will make the necessary arrangements with the Duchess. Say we convene on the front lawn tomorrow at ten?"

Hawthorne smiled back, baring his perfectly aligned teeth, which James had the sudden urge to knock clean out. "Until then, Stanton."

James swirled his drink and contemplated the viscount's retreating back.

To look at them, no one would've suspected he and Hawthorne had just arranged to come at each other with the sharpest of implements in the express hope of drawing blood, winning the fair maiden in the process.

Hawthorne was heading straight for Miranda, so James downed his brandy and placed the glass on the sideboard.

He'd stomached enough for one evening and witnessing another round of Miranda and the viscount's tedious courtship rituals would hardly aid in his digestion.

In any case, he needed to rest up for the morrow's bloodletting.

Miranda watched the viscount's approach with no little trepidation.

She wasn't sure what had just passed between him and James, but from the charged looks they'd exchanged, it didn't bode well.

All evening, she'd made a concerted effort to appear calm, pushing what had happened upstairs to the back of her mind with everything else she had yet to contend with. Yet she couldn't escape her feelings of guilt as she looked to the viscount's unsuspecting face.

"Miss Drayton. Would you care for a turn of the room?"

She rallied a smile and took his arm. "Certainly, my lord."

Walking past the sofa, she spied James' retreat from the room, and the tension left her shoulders.

Saved from his boorish glares, she could better maintain her composure. Though, it could be argued that his censure was the least of what she deserved.

"How are you enjoying the house party so far?" Lord Hawthorne enquired, drawing back her attention.

Of course, if she hadn't allowed her attention to waver in the first place, she wouldn't be in this predicament.

"It has certainly proved eventful," she said. "My aunt's no novice when it comes to entertaining as I'm sure you would agree."

"Indeed, though it must be said, some aspects have been more pleasant than others. But you needn't despair as I have everything well in hand. Stanton will no longer be bothering you. Of that, you may rest assured."

Miranda swallowed.

What on earth had happened between James and the viscount back there?

But Lord Hawthorne took himself off before she could bring herself to ask.

28

Sabers at Sunlight

The world had gone mad. Well and truly insane. Else, Miranda had gone to her bed last night in civilized 1813 only to have awakened in feudal times.

Who challenged a fellow peer to a 'friendly fencing bout' on a Dowager Duchess' front lawn these days? Lord Hawthorne, apparently, and all supposedly in *her* honor.

Well, Miranda certainly wouldn't want anyone falling on their sword for her sake.

If only she'd pressed the viscount for details last night, then she may well have prevented the bout altogether. Though to be fair, who would've thought Lord Hawthorne's choice method for 'dealing' with a potential rival was to come at them, swords blazing?

Joining the others around the makeshift arena, Miranda realized she belonged to the minority. For apart from her mother—who was twisting her handkerchief in her hands and looking decidedly anxious—her fellow spectators were clearly impatient for the duel to begin. As if this were some great lark. Had they no forethought, nor a care? Someone could get seriously maimed, even killed!

She scoured the crowd for her father and spied him inspecting the weaponry, the colonel having volunteered to serve as the referee.

Setting a path towards him, she hoped the swords he wielded weren't as sharp as they appeared.

"Father, you must call a halt to this nonsense at once," she insisted without preamble.

The colonel glanced up in bemusement. "Stop the duel? Whyever would I wish to do that, my girl? With all those dandified namby-pambies galivanting about Town, I'd seriously lost all faith in our sex. A disgrace, that's what they are! But Stanton and Hawthorne...now they're *real* men. Men I could've used in Portugal, let me tell you."

"But Papa, the duel," Miranda said, thinking to appeal to his softer side. "Someone could get hurt..."

The colonel's smile was relentless as he looked down the length of the blade. "That's precisely the point, my dear."

Miranda revised her opinion.

The whole world hadn't gone mad, just its male contingent. Had they all been dropped on their heads as babes?

Still, she couldn't let up with so much at stake. "If not for that, Father, then think of the scandal."

Considering Lady Whincup's expression, news of the bout would be all over Town before they even set a foot back in London.

"That my daughter inspired a duel between two of the most eligible bachelors of the ton? Why, I have never been so proud!" the colonel declared, laying down the first sword and then reaching for the other.

Miranda shook her head and left him to it. His was obviously a hopeless case. She then headed for the most rational person she knew. The person who she should've approached from the onset as her opinion held the most sway.

"Aunt Bethel," she called out breathlessly. "Put an end to this madness, I implore you."

The Dowager Duchess turned and frowned. "Calm yourself, dear girl. There's no cause for alarm. James and Lord Hawthorne are skilled swordsmen who can handle themselves. I wouldn't allow the bout otherwise. Why not relax and enjoy the spectacle."

Miranda gritted her teeth.

How was she supposed to *relax* when she was in real danger of losing her breakfast all over her aunt's ruby slippers?

A cheer rose from the crowd, and Miranda turned as James and Lord Hawthorne entered the designated arena.

James flashed a grin and casually removed his jacket, handing it to a nearby footman. He then rolled up his shirt sleeves, looking decidedly unconcerned about the bloodshed that would surely follow.

The colonel handed James his sword and he raised it in the air, eliciting another cheer from the spectators.

Lord Hawthorne was more circumspect, taking James' measure as he tested the weight of his own weapon and waited for the signal to begin.

James smiled at the viscount as they faced each other off, then darted Miranda a glance, having the audacity to wink at her!

Miranda grabbed her aunt's arm. "Please, Aunt. Someone is bound to be hurt. The imbeciles aren't even wearing protective padding, for goodness' sake!"

If James were injured, or worse, she would do him in herself!

The Dowager Duchess placed a hand over Miranda's own. "Breathe easy, my girl," she said. "The only thing in danger of being damaged here is male pride, and that's never a bad thing by my estimation. Let the men resolve their differences in their own way. Archaic perhaps, but ever so entertaining for the rest of us."

Miranda clasped her hands together and watched as her father approached the combatants.

A hush settled over the lawn. The colonel called out *En Garde*, and the men raised their swords.

Then there was nothing left to do but hold her breath.

James narrowed his gaze onto Hawthorne.

He may have put on a cavalier front for the ladies, but he was entirely focused. This was serious—deadly serious—and there was no way in blazes that he was going to let the viscount win.

Predictably, Hawthorne launched into a blistering attack, which James rode out, easily deflecting each blow. He even went so far as to goad, "Is that all you've got?" when the viscount was close enough to feel James breathing down his neck.

Hawthorne snarled. "Your arrogance will be the cause of your downfall one of these days, Stanton."

"Oh, I don't doubt it," James replied, twisting out of the viscount's hold and launching a surprise attack of his own. "But unfortunately for you, this won't be the day."

He smiled to see a bead of sweat drip off the end of the viscount's angular nose. But his expression soon hardened as the viscount suddenly veered to James' left, missing his arm by an inch.

James scowled as he unleashed a compound attack, grunting each time their swords clashed.

They were both breathing heavily now, and James rolled his shoulders to feel his shirt clinging to his back.

"You think Miss Drayton wants your attentions, Stanton?" the viscount taunted. "I assure you she doesn't appreciate them. Neither do I, so leave my intended be!"

"So she's your intended now," James said, sidestepping the viscount's lunge to avoid being sliced clean open. "Did I somehow miss the announcement?"

"Any day now," Hawthorne hissed. "And once it's official, I'll expect you to bow out gracefully. If you can manage it."

"Oh, I'll bow out *gracefully*," James said. "On the odd chance you manage to win Miranda's hand."

"That's Miss Drayton to you," the viscount corrected. "And be assured, my ring on her finger will be all the verification you need."

James spun around and met Hawthorne's blade at full pelt. "We'll see, shall we? Winner takes all in any event."

Then James spotted an opening, lunging forward and nicking the viscount's forearm with the tip of his blade.

The colonel raised his hand and called an end to the match.

"Well done, gentleman," he said, applauding loudly as he entered the field. "You certainly put on a rousing display. Although, there can only be one victor in the end."

James raised his sword, and the spectators cheered as he took a bow. He then put his saber aside to shake the viscount's hand.

"A fair match, Stanton," Hawthorne said. "Your footwork's quite impressive."

"You certainly put me through my paces," James returned in kind. "In fact, I believe I may have enjoyed myself, thus wouldn't be averse to a rematch someday."

The viscount eyed him sardonically. "I never say never, but I trust the next we meet will be under more congenial circumstances."

James returned Hawthorne gaze and begrudged him a certain measure of respect.

The man was only protecting what he thought was his. An inclination James could well understand.

The moment passed as a torrent of well-wishers inundated the field. James searched for Miranda, but she wasn't amongst them.

Freddy's sisters were the first to reach them.

"You were magnificent, Lord Stanton," the younger sibling, Sarah, declared. "Like a knight from stories of olde! Oh, and you equipped yourself well, Lord Hawthorne," she added hastily, her cheeks coloring as she looked to the viscount.

The elder sister, Annabel, bypassed James completely, rushing to Hawthorne's side. "Are you pained, my lord?" she asked, giving the viscount a thorough once over.

Hawthorne looked at his arm as if only remembering the injury. "It's nothing," he said. "A scratch at best."

Hawthorne's look turned mystified as Annabel reached into her reticule for her handkerchief and applied it to the wound. Lucinda appeared with a clean bandage, which Annabel used to bind the viscount's arm, tying the ends into a neat bow.

"There." Annabel stepped back and admired her handiwork. "Be sure to get it properly cleaned, though."

The viscount, still looking more than a little perplexed, mumbled his thanks.

James bit back a smile.

Hawthorne probably wasn't accustomed to being fussed over, so it was amusing to see him flounder as a result. Whether it was the viscount's intention or not, his reputation as a tedious bore may very well suffer due to their morning's swordplay.

And how telling that Annabel had been the one to rush over and tend to the viscount's wounds whilst Miranda was playing least in sight.

The Dowager Duchess arrived then, flanked by a couple of capable-looking footmen. The first carried a wad of fresh towels, the second, a tray of glasses.

James gratefully accepted an offering from each.

His godmother reached for a glass and raised it. "That was some display of prowess, my boy. Indeed, I'm so over-come that I'm almost lost for words."

James' lips twisted at the 'almost' part. "At least someone was impressed," he said.

"Allow her some time," the Dowager Duchess sounded. "But you can take comfort in knowing that my niece was so concerned, she was bent on preventing the bout altogether."

James scoffed. "Worried for whom, Godmother? Me or her dear viscount? Although, if she were as overwrought as you say, you'd think she would've tarried long enough to check on our welfare."

"I wouldn't be so hasty to judge. Things are often more complicated than they seem, especially when it comes to one's emotions," she said.

James sighed.

When he'd envisioned how his godmother's house party would play out, he hadn't expected a farce that even Shake-speare would envy.

He raised his glass to his lips and almost lost his claret completely as Freddy slapped him on the shoulder.

"Good show, old chum. No denying who's top dog now, hmm?"

James carefully lowered his glass. "That wasn't my inten-tion, I assure you. The viscount and I decided to put on a show for the ladies, nothing more. And considering how the match played out, Hawthorne is equally a winner in my book."

Freddy snorted. "If a friendly bout was all it was, then I moonlight as an acrobat at Vauxhall on my spare evenings."

"Ah-ha," James said in mock insight. "So that's your secret, Lord Twinkle-Toes."

Freddy raised his glass. "*Touché, mon ami, touché.*" He was the first to admit to being cursed with not two but three left feet.

James downed his wine as Freddy surveyed the crowd.

"So, where is our lovely lady of the moment?" he asked.

James swallowed before replying. "She left."

Freddy raised his brows. "Unsporting of her, don't you think? Considering this was all for her benefit."

James was proud to pull off an indifferent shrug. "I'm sure she has her reasons."

"Women!" Freddy said it like a curse. "Hardly worth the hassle, I say."

James nodded even though he didn't particularly agree.

Whilst his interactions with Miranda couldn't be described as easy, he wouldn't give her up for the world.

He looked to the manor and wondered where she could've gotten to.

He'd defeated Hawthorne as he knew he would, yet it turned out to be a hollow victory in the end.

What was success without having someone at your side to share in the spoils?

Hours passed before James could escape. The celebrations turned into a festival of sorts, with his godmother ordering a tent to be erected and a feast laid out underneath. Then came the music, courtesy of the Dowager Duchess' head groom and his trusty fiddle.

And all throughout, Miranda remained markedly absent.

29

The Decision

As expected, conversation at dinner centered on the morning's fencing match. This despite the post-bout revelry stretching well past noon.

Whilst Miranda was glad the affair had ended without serious injury, she'd been in no mood to celebrate.

She'd spent the entire match on tenterhooks, unable to tear her gaze away. And when the viscount almost sliced James' arm clean through, the only thing that prevented Miranda from charging onto the field and putting an end to the bout herself was her aunt's restraining hand on her elbow.

Only after James had been declared champion could she breathe freely again, and she'd been close to tears so great was her relief. Relief that *James* was unharmed, never mind the viscount.

That was when it had hit her.

How could she even think of marrying Lord Hawthorne when she was still completely, madly, *dreadfully* in love with James?

The simple truth being she couldn't.

It wouldn't be fair to any of them.

At the sound of approaching voices in the hall, Miranda turned to the parlor door and caught Lord Hawthorne's eye as he entered the room.

He headed toward her. "Miss Drayton, I'm so pleased that you were able to join us for dinner."

The Dowager Duchess had attributed Miranda's absence to a headache brought on by all the excitement, which was a fair enough excuse.

Better than the truth in any case.

"I was sorry to miss the celebrations so could hardly forego dinner as well," she said. "How are you holding up? Is the arm bothering you?"

He smiled self-deprecatingly. "No, not at all. My pride's bruised more than anything for leaving myself wide open like that. But then, Stanton was the better swordsman on the day, as much as I loathe to say it."

Miranda returned his smile, though hers felt strained.

The viscount was truly an honorable man. And here she was about to dash his hopes like the poor excuse for a match she'd turned out to be.

Her distress must have been shown on her face, for the viscount drew her to a quiet corner of the room.

"What is it, Miss Drayton? Your head's not troubling you again, I hope."

Miranda shook her head.

It wasn't her head—her heart more like. Not to mention her prickling conscience.

"I was just wondering whether you've approached my father."

The viscount looked surprised. "Not as yet. But I intend to pay him a call when we get back to London, so you needn't worry."

She placed her hand on his sleeve. "Please don't."

A terrible silence followed as the viscount measured her words.

"You're saying you no longer welcome my suit?" he finally said.

Miranda closed her eyes and nodded.

"I see."

She took a deep breath, knowing an explanation was in order. "I'm so sorry, Lord Hawthorne. I did intend to go through with it. Rather, what I mean to say is—"

"It's Stanton, isn't it?" he stated flatly.

Miranda didn't respond as she could hardly deny it.

"Are you sure? Almost anyone else and I might understand. But *Stanton*?"

"I'm afraid so," she returned with a humorless laugh. "If only it wasn't the case."

Lord Hawthorne's gaze shifted to some point behind her right shoulder. She didn't turn, though.

If she looked at James, it would only make what she had to say the more harrowing.

"I hope you're not too disappointed, my lord. Please believe me when I say I had no intention of hurting you."

Lord Hawthorne turned back, his expression softening. "Think nothing of it. We cannot have the future viscountess pining for another, can we? Besides, whilst there's bound to be talk, no formal announcement has been made, nor any documents signed. Thus, I expect we'll emerge from this relatively unscathed."

"You are a good man, Lord Hawthorne."

He dipped his head closer. "I appreciate the sentiment, my dear. But please don't go bandying it about as I've a reputation to uphold."

Miranda laughed as he stood back and bowed. "I wish you well for the future, my lady. Only a brave woman would dare to take Stanton on."

"Either that or a foolish one."

They exchanged farewells and Miranda let out a sigh.

Whilst probably the most difficult thing she'd ever done, the discussion had gone better than she'd expected.

What to do about James wasn't so straight forward, though.

Rallying herself, she turned. But the man she was seeking was no longer in the room. Then the grandfather clock chimed midnight.

Whether as a good omen or not remained to be seen.

James may be partial to kissing her, but that could very well be the extent of it. Miranda wasn't so naïve to believe he held any deeper feelings for her.

Lord Hawthorne thought her brave, and it would take a whole lot of gumption to ask James the one question she feared the most.

As talk of early starts and long journeys permeated the room, she went to follow the other guests into the hall.

Her aunt hailed her by the door. "Ah, there's my elusive niece."

Miranda attempted a smile. "Aunt Bethel, you must be beside yourself. This year's house party is sure to be the talk of the town, for the next sennight at least."

The Dowager Duchess' lips twisted wryly. "Thank you, my dear. I must say I'm more than a little pleased with how the gathering turned out. Although this morning's bout will be almost impossible to top. Perhaps I should make this fencing tournament an annual occurrence. That would certainly draw in a crowd. It's a shame you missed all the celebrations."

"You all appeared to be having such a merry time of it, I doubt my absence was even noted."

"Appearances can be deceiving," the Dowager Duchess said. "I know of at least two gentlemen who felt your absence most keenly."

Miranda swallowed uncomfortably, and her aunt sighed. "I understand why you felt you couldn't stay, though. But now you've had time to consider matters, have you come to a decision?"

"I informed Lord Hawthorne that I couldn't marry him," Miranda told her. "But how I'm to go on from here is still up for debate."

"I'm glad you made your feelings known. As for my god-son, hear him out and trust everything will follow from there. Don't be afraid to go after what you want. Even heart-break is preferable to a lifetime of 'what ifs.'"

"Thank you, Aunt," Miranda said, even though heart-break was the one thing she'd been trying to avoid from the very beginning.

But then, she'd already learned how to live with a broken heart, hadn't she?

"Sleep well, my dear, and remember, things will un-doubtedly look brighter in the morning."

Miranda kissed her aunt's cheek and left the drawing room, praying her aunt was right.

***

Despite her exhaustion, Miranda was wide awake in bed not two hours later.

Lying quietly in the dark, she'd given her thoughts free rein, and she couldn't sleep for picking over every interac-tion she'd had with James since his return, which only left her the more confounded.

She tossed off the bedclothes in exasperation and reached for her dressing gown.

Belting the gown around her waist, she opened her bed-room door and slipped into the hall.

If she found the most uninteresting book of her aunt's collection, she might be able to bore herself to sleep.

Downstairs, she headed straight toward the library, where she hovered in the doorway.

James was on the sofa contemplating the flames in the fireplace.

He looked delightfully disheveled, having discarded his jacket over a nearby chair, and his hair was in disarray as if he'd passed his fingers through it a few too many times.

She took a tentative step forward, and he turned, slowly rising to his feet.

For an indefinable time, they just stared at each other.

Then they spoke at once.

"Mira—"

James—"

Miranda laughed to cover the awkwardness. "Don't let me disturb you. I can see that you're exhausted after the day you've had. Congratulations, by the by. You certainly made an impression this morning. I even heard one of the ladies crown you the 'McBane of Hampshire,' which is high praise indeed."

"I thought you opposed the match. Now you're offering me your felicitations?"

Miranda felt her color rising. "Yes, well, you were fortunate not to be hurt, and the viscount suffering merely a scratch—and all for what? The sake of foolish pride."

"Oh, it involved a bit more than that as I'm sure you're aware," he returned, stepping closer. "Why did you flee afterwards?"

She averted her gaze.

If she answered, she'd reveal too much.

"Mira, would you look at me? Please?"

Raising her eyes, she blurted the first thing that came to mind. "You left the parlor early this evening."

James smiled a little as he said, "There's only so much a man can take when he sees the woman he wants above all else in intimate conversation with another."

Miranda sucked in a breath.

Did he mean...?

James placed his hands in his pockets, else he'd pull Miranda in his arms if only to prove that she was indeed real.

Hadn't he just been thinking of her and suddenly she appeared in her flowing nightclothes as if stepping straight from his dreams?

He'd pretty much given up hope. Over the course of the house party, Miranda had made her preference for Hawthorne more than clear. And the worst of it was James couldn't begrudge her choice. Hawthorne was deuced near perfect, the quintessential gentleman by all accounts. One just had to look at how magnanimous he was in defeat.

In effect, he was everything James was not.

And yet, Miranda was here, and the viscount nowhere to be seen. And for once, she didn't look to have one foot out the door.

Feeling emboldened, he stepped closer and was heartened when she didn't pull away.

Had she rethought her decision to wed Hawthorne?

Well, he'd never know unless he asked.

"Are you still intent on marrying the viscount?" he said gruffly.

She slowly shook her head.

Not exactly the adamant denial he was looking for. "Do you mean, 'no, I don't intend to marry him,' or you just don't know?"

"Just no," she whispered.

James released his breath.

He took her hand and placed it over his heart, covering it with his own. "Well, that's something," he said, "and there's something else you should know. I came back for one reason only, and that reason was you."

Her breath caught. "What? Why now?"

James rubbed his thumb against the back of her hand. "Before you surprised me under the mistletoe that blessed Christmas, I'd already decided. I wouldn't be beholden to anyone, especially no female. Not after seeing how my mother's death all but destroyed my father."

"James—" Her eyes were troubled as she raised her other hand to his chest.

"Please allow me to finish while I still can."

At her nod, he continued. "As I was saying, dear girl, when you kissed me that night, I quickly realized I wasn't in any way near as impenetrable as I thought. How easily you slipped through my defenses and completely undid me with one little kiss!"

She frowned. "But to hear you talk, the kiss didn't mean a thing."

"Oh, it meant so little that I was scared witless, and I couldn't face it—or you—for three long years. Not without seriously questioning everything I thought I wanted. But when I heard you were set on Hawthorne, I couldn't escape it any longer. It's you I wanted, *want*. It's always been you. Only you."

Her look turned incredulous. "I had no idea."

"That was the whole point." He lifted his hands to cup her jaw. "You, my darling woman, are my worst nightmare come to life. You somehow managed to insinuate yourself into my every thought, my every desire, not to mention my very heart, and I wouldn't have it any other way. I love you." He gazed deeply into her eyes as he waited for his words to sink in. "And dare I ask whether you feel the same for me?"

"Of course I love you, you fool. I always have."

She seized his shirtfront and crushed her lips to his.

He accepted the onslaught with relish.

They'd embraced before, but never with such *feeling*. Like they were trying to pack three years of wasted opportunity into one meeting of lips.

She moaned and James took back control, plying her with kisses, each longer and more luscious than the one before. He spun them around, bringing her against the nearest bookshelf.

Not near enough.

Grabbing fistfuls of her nightgown in his hands, he groaned to feel the heat of her core brush against his thigh, his leg somehow having made its way in between hers.

He tore his lips from her mouth and redirected his attention to her neck.

She writhed against him. "James, I want...I need..."

He eased back and gazed into her eyes.

Her pupils were so dilated, he could've easily lost himself in them for days.

But there was plenty of time for that *after* they wed.

"I know, sweetheart," he said, smoothing her nightdress back down. "I want you too, and how I long to show you precisely how much. But I'm determined to get at least one thing right." He stroked a stray tendril of hair from her face and hooked it behind her ear. "I've a few things to organize, then I'll be back to speak with your father. It should only take a day or two. If that pleases you, of course."

Her responding smile spoke volumes "Nothing could thrill me more. Well, almost nothing."

"Ah, Mira, you would test the fortitude of a saint, so what chance does a mere mortal like me have?" With considerable effort, he stepped back, taking her hand and interlacing their fingers. "Come. I best get you to bed before I'm tempted to toss all my good intentions into the fireplace."

She playfully bumped into his side on their way to the door. "And when did you become so noble, my lord?"

James grinned, though he was being entirely earnest when he said, "As it so happened, one lonely winter's night this angel appeared to me—"

30

Never Forgotten

B ack in Mayfair, life resumed pretty much as usual—if one discounted the fact Miranda was still abed as the clock struck noon.

Since the colonel hadn't been too pleased to hear that an offer from Lord Hawthorne wouldn't be forthcoming, Miranda had taken to breaking her fast in her room.

She could hardly tell her father that she'd overthrown the viscount for James, especially as she didn't know when—*or if*—James would return with an offer of his own.

He said he'd only be a couple of days. But when two days turned into three, then four, and now stretching into five, Miranda had started to worry. What if he'd changed his mind? He may indeed love her—he certainly sounded sincere at the time. Yet was love enough to overcome a lifetime of misgivings?

Now that Miranda knew why he'd left all those years before, she wasn't so sure.

She pushed her toast aside and went to rise from the bed. But seeing her bedroom door swing open, she sank back down and scooped up the tray just as Lucinda catapulted herself onto the mattress.

"Good, you're awake," Lucinda said. "You've really got this lounging about like a queen down pat. I must say I'm mightily impressed. Still, you missed *Miss M's* latest edition this morning, so I thought I'd bring it to you."

Miranda took the periodical and placed it on the bedside table with her half-eaten breakfast.

Lucinda frowned at the discarded papers, then back at Miranda. "You know, Mira, there's a world of difference between languishing and withering dead away. You are barely eating, showing no interest in anything... Continue at this rate and you'll be nothing but a sallow waif when James comes a-calling. And you wouldn't want to swoon at his feet before he even gets to his grand declaration!"

When Miranda had told her family that she wasn't to marry the viscount, Lucinda hadn't let up until she'd wrangled the full story from her.

Miranda had made sure to glaze over certain details, though.

"We don't even know if James is coming back," she lamented.

Lucinda tutted. "Of course, he's coming back, you ninny. He said as much, didn't he? And I think we can trust he's a man of his word. Regardless, I have a feeling that today's the day."

"You said that yesterday."

"Perhaps, but the feeling's much stronger today." Lucinda leaped from the bed and outstretched her hand. "Come on. For all we know, James is on his way over right this instant, and that old flannel you persist in wearing won't do at all."

Miranda allowed herself to be drawn to her feet and they called for Abigail.

After Miranda was dressed, they went down to the drawing room to wait until it was time for their afternoon callers.

As expected, tales of the fencing bout had spread like an ague, resulting in an influx of visitors to Drayton House, much to their mother's dismay.

It was all anyone could talk about: Lord Hawthorne's supposed disfigurement, which explained his sudden flight to Devon instead of returning to Town with his father. And Lucinda certainly hadn't helped to dispel the rumors, cheerily confirming to all and sundry that James had indeed been the first to draw blood.

With all the nodding and smiling, Miranda's head was pounding by the time their last callers left the parlor. So she went by the conservatory to the back garden, seeking solace.

Now, the gardens at Drayton House were hardly comparable to those of Rose Manor. But their gardener had created an oasis within the space he'd been allotted, planting beds of foxgloves, peonies, and Sweet William between the interlacing pathways that led to the three-tiered fountain at the center.

Miranda took the main path, trailing her hand along the jasmine hedge as she went.

Despite the peaceful surrounds, her fears still loomed like dark clouds on the horizon.

If James didn't come, whatever would she do?

"Ouch!" She glared down at her finger; the tip having caught on a particularly angry barb.

"Here, allow me." James appeared out of nowhere and brought her finger to his mouth.

Miranda blinked. "You came."

She didn't quite believe James was in her garden, let alone tending to her wound in such a manner.

In fact, she was enjoying his unique type of tendering so much, she mewled in protest when he withdrew her finger from his mouth to say, "You doubted that I would?"

"Yes, no...*oh*, I don't know."

She could barely think straight, what with his thumb circling her palm in a such a fashion.

Ordering herself to focus, she looked to his lips. But then she only wondered how long she had to wait before he kissed her again.

"I will never willingly leave your side again," he said. "It was difficult enough the first time, believe me. I was delayed by the archbishop, who happened to be on sabbatical in Bristol of all places. Then I had to confer with the family jeweler before I could give you this."

He reached into his jacket pocket and retrieved a small box. Sinking onto one knee, he opened the lid to reveal the sparkling emerald ring nestled inside.

"Mira, my love, you must realize how much I adore you. You would make me the happiest of men if you would put me out of my misery and consent to be my bride."

Miranda couldn't speak for being so choked up with tears.

How she'd dreamed of this day for so long.

James shot to his feet and pulled her into his arms. "Oh, sweetheart." He swiped away her tears with his thumb. "I cannot bear to see you cry. Tell me they're happy tears at least."

She nodded, her vision blurry as he swam in and out of focus.

"Then it's a 'yes'?"

"Yes, a million times, yes!" she managed to say, wrapping her arms around his shoulders.

"At last." He took her hand and slipped his ring onto her third finger. "There, I knew my mother's ring would suit you perfectly."

She smiled, allowing all she was feeling to shine through her eyes. "I love you."

"And I you, my darling girl." He dipped his head to kiss her as he did best.

Miranda sighed, welcoming him in.

She didn't think she'd ever tire of James wanting her, loving her.

Her dream come true.

James drew Miranda closer, savoring the moment.

He'd been awfully nervous earlier, wanting his declaration to be perfect. Miranda deserved nothing less given everything he'd put her through.

Yet against all odds, she'd not only forgiven him for the past but she also accepted him wholeheartedly as only she could.

Thinking of her generous nature, he drew back to ask, "How soon before we can wed?

She pretended to consider it. "How long...hmm, let me see. Three years has a nice ring to it, don't you think?"

"I was thinking more like three days," he said. The special license he'd taken such pains to acquire was burning a hole through his waistcoat pocket. "We've tarried long enough already, wouldn't you agree?"

"*Three days!* That's nowhere near enough time! How about three weeks?"

"A sennight," he countered. "That's my final offer."

"If you insist. Although if your bride turns up dressed in rags, you'll only have yourself to blame."

He grinned. "Honestly, sweetheart, you could wear sackcloth to our wedding, and I wouldn't even blink. Provided you grant me full removal rights after the ceremony, of course. We could have a burning ceremony to mark the occasion."

She slapped his chest. "You are entirely ridiculous, you do realize? Now I'm worried I may have been too hasty in accepting you."

"Too late. You couldn't get rid of me now, even if you tried. But just to be sure, let's make it official by sharing our news with your family, then we can get onto the planning. We've only seven days after all."

She gave him a look. "And whose fault is that?"

He laughed. "Guilty as charged."

On the way back to the house, James' step was as light as his mood.

How was such joy even possible?

Nearing the end of the path, Miranda stopped and pulled him back into the shadows.

"One more thing," she said, then pressed a hard kiss to his mouth.

"What was that for?" he asked some time afterwards.

"For coming back to me," she said solemnly.

He cupped her cheek. "I will always return to you, Mira. That I can promise."

31

His Vision in White

James knew he was stalking the perimeter of the Drayton's front parlor with a silly grin plastered over his face. But frankly, he didn't give a toss.

In mere minutes, Miranda would walk through that door and finally become his, and he was mightily impatient to get on with it.

They'd kept the guest list short with only Miranda's immediate family, the Dowager Duchess and Meg, Freddy—who'd been chuffed to stand up for James—the Burtons, and the requisite vicar making up the numbers.

James had delayed notifying his stepmother of the nuptials until the last minute, sending her a missive from Miranda's house. As an added precaution, he'd tossed the colonel's footman a crown, suggesting the lad take in some sights along the way. He couldn't risk Muriel turning up uninvited and spoiling their day.

What a glorious day it was too.

Starting back towards the vicar, James wondered at the parlor's transformation.

Rose garlands had been draped from the walls and massive floral arrangements adorned every surface. In fact, if he closed his eyes, the scent alone would mistake him for Rose Manor.

He passed by the seated guests and caught wind of Lucinda's conversation.

"For some reason, Mira adamantly refused a rose arbor," she was saying to Miss Burton. "I could've found an exact replica of the one at Rose Manor for them to marry beneath. It would have been so romantic, but my sister was dead set against it!"

James kept on walking, knowing when one should leave a subject well alone.

"There you are!" the Dowager Duchess said, pulling James to a stop by the fireplace. "And looking mightily pleased with yourself, if I may be so bold to venture."

James snorted. "Since when have you ever shied away from stating your opinion, Godmother?"

She feigned an offended look. "We are all capable of change, my boy. Why, one only needs to look at you and Miranda."

"Oh, I don't think we've changed so much as finally come to the same conclusion."

"However you put it, it certainly took you both long enough!" the Dowager Duchess retorted. "You are indeed fortunate, my boy. But do know, if you take my niece for granted—for even a second—you will find yourself answerable to me."

"Now, now, Your Grace. You're sounding so much like the colonel, one would think you were related."

The Dowager Duchess rolled her eyes. "In all seriousness, James, I am so pleased for you, and I feel right here," she said, bringing her hand to her chest, "that your father would've been ever so proud if he were still with us today."

James cleared his throat, a wave of emotion taking him unawares. "Thank you, dear Godmama. That means everything to me."

"Perhaps not quite everything." Her eyes twinkled as she looked to the door. "For here comes your bride now."

James looked up and swallowed.

Miranda stood framed in the doorway, the light from the hallway casting her in an ethereal glow.

She was draped in a gown of pale silk embroidered with a chain of red roses that spanned her waist before bunching at one hip and falling in a trail to the floor.

He imagined tracing that line with his fingertips. Then again with his lips.

At his godmother's urging, he went and took his position by the vicar, his gaze never leaving his bride.

With excruciating deliberation, the colonel marched Miranda toward him.

When she came to stand beside him, the vicar intoned, "Who giveth this woman to be married to this man?"

"I do." The colonel took Miranda's hand and passed it to James.

Glancing at their clasped hands, James was surprised to find his was shaking. Then Miranda squeezed his fingers, and his unease dissipated.

Looking to the vicar, he made a silent vow.

He'd treasure Miranda till the end of his days.

***

"Happy?" James asked his newly bequeathed wife when they were finally able to snatch a private moment following the ceremony.

The sounds of merrymaking swirled around them, but in that heartbeat, it was as if they were completely alone.

Miranda grinned. "Deliriously so."

He pressed a kiss to her temple. "Even if you weren't so deliriously pleased, I can promise you, sweetheart, you certainly will be very soon."

He then had the delight of watching her blush deepen to a rosy pink.

"Is that so, my lord husband," she said, shooting him a look that only added flames to his heated state.

"You know, I like the sound of that so much, I insist you refer to me as 'your lord husband' from this point onward."

She rolled her eyes. "In your dreams, sirrah."

Catching her gaze, he said, "Oh, most definitely. Every. Single. Night."

Hearing the mantle clock's chime, he reluctantly eased back. "How soon before we can depart?"

She wetted her lips, drawing his attention back to her mouth. "A half hour, mayhap a little sooner?"

"Still too long by my standards, but I guess we'll have to make do."

They rejoined the others and partook in another toast and more cinnamon scrolls, the latter sent with Mrs. Potts' express felicitations.

All the while, James marked the minutes until he could spirit Miranda away and personally welcome her home.

32

All She Ever Wanted

After what seemed like another three years to Miranda, they were finally ensconced in the carriage and making their way to her new home.

The day turned out even better than she could've imagined, the ceremony brief but heartfelt, with only their dearest in attendance to mark the occasion. Now with all the farewells behind them, Miranda was excited to embark on the next phase of her life as James' wife.

His wife.

Hearing James' vow to love and cherish her for the rest of their days had left her feeling giddy and more than a little apprehensive. She knew what to expect when it came to her wedding night—more or less. Her mother had refused to give her any details, though, only saying James would know what he was about and leaving it at that.

She shifted closer to James, and he turned her gently to face him.

"You've no cause for concern," he said. "I vowed to look after you, so look after you I shall. I would do everything in my power to never intentionally hurt you again."

She rallied a smile. "I do realize that, and I adore you the more for it. I just feel jittery all a sudden. Ridiculous, I know."

He rubbed his thumb along the inside of her elbow, which did little to calm her rampaging nerves.

"That's completely understandable. I have to admit to being a mite apprehensive myself. If only you knew how often I have imagined this moment." He hooked a finger on the inside of her glove and rolled the satin down her arm before removing it completely and tossing it aside. He then reached for her hand and kissed her open palm.

She shuddered. "Is that so?" she somehow managed to quip. "Then you must enlighten me, dear husband, as your knowledge is far superior to mine. In this instance only, mind you."

James' pulse leaped as the word 'husband' passed Miranda's lips yet again. Something he doubted he'd ever tire of hearing.

As he looked to his wife—yes, *wife*—it seemed his method of distraction was working. Her focus had shifted from her jitters to how he was making her feel. So he reached for her left hand and dealt with that glove just as deftly as he had with the first.

Baring her arm, he traced his finger down its length to her wrist. "That's precisely my plan," he said, "just as soon as we reach home."

He drew her into a heady kiss—a kiss he'd been awaiting all day.

Now they were wed, they were free to indulge themselves whenever they so desired. And he certainly desired.

The wheels came to a stop, and they jolted apart as the carriage doors swung open.

James shooed the groom aside, stepping out to hand his bride down himself. As they turned toward the townhouse, his enthusiasm dampened. "My only regret is not having Stanton House readied in time."

Miranda looked to the unimposing brick structure in interest. "Honestly, James, this looks positively delightful, and I'm simply happy to be wherever you are."

He let out his breath.

By rights, she should expect all the trimmings that came with being his countess. Yet she seemed to understand his reluctance when it came to reclaiming his childhood home.

How she continued to amaze him.

Catching his bride in his arms, he smiled to hear her squeal of surprise. "I'm determined to start on the right foot," he said, carrying her over the threshold.

Once inside the house, Miranda wriggled as if she wished to be let down, but he didn't budge.

"Ah, Benson." He nodded to his butler who was hovering by the doorway. "May I present my beloved bride, Lady Miranda Stanton."

"My lady." Benson didn't even blink at finding his new mistress in his master's arms.

Although terribly flushed, Miranda's voice was impressively even as she said, "It's a pleasure to meet you, Benson. I am much looking forward to working with you and the rest of the staff."

"There will be plenty of time for introductions later," he quickly put in.

Now he had Miranda where he wanted her, he was unwilling to relinquish her for even a second.

"That will be all, Benson," he said. "Indeed, you and the rest of the staff may consider this your afternoon off."

"As you so wish. Thank you, my lord." Benson bowed before making an unobtrusive exit through a side door.

Smiling to himself, James scaled the staircase, not slowing his pace until he reached his—correction, *their*—bedchamber.

He kicked the door closed with a satisfying thud.

Only then did he release Miranda, lowering her down his body until her feet landed softly on the rug. "Here we are, my lady. Home at last."

As Miranda took in her new surrounds, James headed for the bottle of champagne chilling on the sideboard. Benson's doing, he didn't doubt. He'd make sure to give the old retainer a well-deserved raise.

He topped the two accompanying glasses with wine, watching Miranda askance.

He hoped she liked what she saw seeing he planned to keep her busy here for quite some time.

An eternity if he could manage it.

He moved back to her side and handed her a glass. "To us. The happiest couple in England, if not the entire world."

Miranda sipped her wine, then slanted a look to the bed. "Has there been...what I mean to say is, has anyone else...?" She shuddered to a stop.

"No. You are the only woman to set foot in this room. Well, apart from the maids, of course."

His attempt at levity fell flat, so he took her glass and placed the crystal flutes to one side, then drew her back into his arms.

"Mira, you truly have made me the happiest of men."

"I feel the exact same way," she replied. "Well, apart from the male part, obviously."

He would never tire of that expression. The one she reserved especially for him.

He dipped his head until his lips were a hairbreadth away. "I think it's long past time I show you how much you mean to me."

Her answer was a drugging kiss, and he delighted in taking the champagne bubbles from her lips and her tongue.

She tasted both tart and sweet. An intoxicating combination.

He didn't let up until she sighed in surrender.

Tugging at the fastenings on the back of her gown, he gruffly asked her to turn.

She gave him her back, so he made quick work of the remaining buttons. He stood back and watched the gown fall to her feet in a silky puddle.

When she made a move to turn back around, he placed his hands on her shoulders. "Wait." He bent to kiss the nape of her neck and unlaced her stays, humming his approval when her corset bounced soundlessly on the rug.

She breathed out in a great rush and James lost all his air entirely.

She wasn't wearing any drawers. Only the sheerest barrier of her shift remained.

He quickly shrugged off his jacket, then traced her delicate spine through the gauzy material.

Seeing her shiver, he impatiently flicked the straps off her shoulders and watched with satisfaction as her shift joined the growing pile of garments on the floor.

"James?" She shot him a tentative lock from over her shoulder.

"Hmm-mmm," was his distracted response.

He trailed his lips along her spine, following the exact path his fingers had taken. Then he dropped to his knees to place an open-mouthed kiss at the base of her spine before spinning her around to extend another just south of her navel.

She quivered, so he grasped her hips in support.

"You are so beautiful," he breathed, meeting her half-lidded gaze from his place of reverence at her feet.

Without breaking eye contact, he reached down to remove her slippers, then traced her feet through her stockings, passing his fingers over the curve of her calves and brushing the insides of her knees.

When his fingers reached the blue ribbons encircling her milky thighs, she gasped, and her legs gave way completely.

He caught her in his arms and carried her to the bed, laying her gently across the satin coverlet.

Standing back, he relished the sight. Miranda draped across his bed in nothing more than her silk stockings.

His fantasy in the flesh.

"No fair," she said. "You are wearing far too many clothes in comparison."

He smiled. "An oversight that can be easily rectified, my lady wife."

He quickly removed his cravat and waistcoat and tossed them to the floor.

She sat up, reaching for the buttons of his shirt. But her fingers were too shaky to be of much use, so he gently brushed them aside. "Here, allow me."

Dispensing with his shirt, he felt himself flush as she stared at his torso.

He stepped between her long legs, reached up to extract the pins from her hair, and watched the silky tresses fall where they may.

She put her hands to his chest.

"Mira," he groaned. He cradled her head through the soft curtain of her hair and tilted her chin toward him. "What your touch does to me, love. I want you so much, positively adore you, in fact," he murmured between open-mouthed kisses.

She grabbed his shoulders, pulling him on top of her. "Then show me, Husband."

He brought their hips together with a guttural moan.

Mine, all mine.

The words reverberated in his head as her wandering fingers left their mark on every dip and contour of his back.

When she reached around to the fall of his waistband, he sucked in a breath.

"I think these have to go as well," she said boldly.

With a rough laugh, James sat back and kicked off his boots, then he removed his trousers and smalls in one clean swipe.

Toppling back onto her, he shuddered to feel her full length pressed against his naked flesh.

They fit perfectly together. Like they were meant to be.

"James," she whispered, looking a little uncertain.

He held her wide green gaze. "Don't think, just feel." He dipped his head, kissing her tenderly before moving to her temple.

He paused to nuzzle behind her ear before trailing his lips along the side of her neck, lingering at that sweet spot between her shoulder and neck. Then he moved down her torso and hovered by her breast.

He didn't rush, tickling the underside of her soft flesh with his nose.

Only when she arched her back did he take the rosy peak into his mouth and suckled her nipple most attentively before switching to the other side.

She moaned whilst his hand went on its own journey, exploring her soft belly, brushing over the curve of her hip, then angling back towards to her darkened curls.

He stilled, raising his head to watch her expression as he gently parted her thighs.

"James!" she cried out when he found her center.

He slowly traced the outer lips of her sex, learning her shape and smiling to find her already hot and wet for him.

Miranda moaned, her eyes widening when he found that elusive spot and began to circle it with slow precision.

She latched onto his biceps and began to move against his hand.

Seeing her lost in passion only made him want her the more.

Relentless, he toyed with her bud, varying his pressure and pace in response to her writhes and moans.

She grasped desperately at his shoulders, her fingernails digging into his skin.

"Mira," he exclaimed, "*Christ almighty!*"

Suddenly, he had to taste her, so he dipped his head and replaced his fingers with his mouth.

He licked her tentatively at first, then more boldly when she didn't shy away.

He looked up. She was watching him, her bottom lip caught between her teeth.

Not about to leave his beloved hanging, he found her sweet spot again, sucking gently then with more intensity until she rewarded him by bucking against his mouth. And when she was close, so tantalizingly close, he used the tip of his tongue to send her hurtling over the edge.

Miranda could do little but gasp as James drew wave after wave of undulated pleasure from her body.

She'd never imagined such a thing to be possible.

Once her tremors had subsided, she pulled him in close. "What on earth was that?"

He smiled, looking immensely pleased with himself. "That, sweetheart, was bliss. Pure bliss."

"But..." She frowned.

Whilst she felt delightfully airy and sated, he obviously hadn't reached the same state.

He chuckled. "But that's not all. Not by a long shot."

He took her lips in another searing kiss, which had her blood stirring anew.

She moved her hands to his back, slowly tracing her fingers along the indentations of his spine until she found the rise of his buttocks. She boldly clasped him, pulling him down to where she needed him most—right where his fingers and tongue had just been.

"Lud, yes!" he exclaimed, griding his hips into hers. "You're so ready," he rasped against her ear. "I'm not sure if I can wait much longer. I'll do my utmost to be gentle, though."

Miranda was well past caring by that point, the roughness of his tone only upping her excitement to a level that demanded immediate satisfaction.

She dug her fingernails into his backside, hoping to convey her urgency.

He entered her then, and she froze.

"Easy, sweetheart." He brushed his lips across her cheek. "It will get better, I promise."

She didn't quite believe him. But surprisingly, when she let herself go, it didn't feel so bad. And when she started to move...

"Yes, love, that's it," he encouraged, plunging deeper and faster until Miranda could've sworn she were flying.

And he was right there with her, convulsing when he too found his release.

"Mira," he breathed, falling off to the side and gathering her in close. "How I love you."

She stroked back his hair, looking across only to find he'd already fallen asleep.

"And how I love you, dear heart," she whispered.

Snuggling into his chest, she smiled, marveling at how she managed to get the earl she'd wanted all along.

Epilogue

THE PAST REVISITED - ROSE MANOR, CHRISTMAS EVE, 1813

Miranda stood wrapped in her husband's warm embrace as they awaited her aunt's grandfather clock to herald Christmas morn.

The last sixth months had flown by, with them dividing their time between Kent and London.

They'd decided to keep the townhouse as it was more than sufficient for their needs. Indeed, she'd grown fond of what James liked to call their illustrious love nest, where he seemed to delight in catching her in their bedchamber with remarkable regularity. Not that she would ever complain.

She had fallen equally in love with Stanton Hall, James' family set reminding her of Rose Manor, though the gardens were in dire need of some tendering. As such, she was more than happy to make their home in Kent, returning to Town when only need be.

As things stood, they had no immediate plans to reclaim Stanton House. Miranda didn't think it fair to eject James' stepfamily from their home, at least not until they required the extra room. Mayhap, not even then.

She placed a hand over her belly and smiled.

She would never expect James to return to the place which held so many unhappy memories, especially now they were well on their way to creating their own family.

"You seem awfully pleased with yourself, Wife," the person she loved above all murmured against her ear. He put his hand over hers and drew her more securely against him. "And how's our little Mirabel doing this evening?"

"Little *Jimmy* is doing just fine," she retorted, turning in his arms to face him. He dipped his head, so she raised her hand to cover his mouth. "Not yet. We must wait for the perfect moment."

"You are perfect," he rumbled against her palm.

Miranda rolled her eyes even though she was secretly thrilled.

The clock chimed twelve and she dropped her hand. "Merry Christmas, J—"

Her sentence was cut short by her husband's lips, his kiss quickly surpassing her first fumbled attempt all those years before.

She settled into his familiar caresses, playfully tugging at his bottom lip until he pulled back with a growl.

"Would you like me to show you what I longed to do to you that fateful night?" he said roughly.

She met his heated look with one of her own. "Please, go right ahead."

She was giddy just at the thought.

Within a flash, James had her back pressed against the sturdy timepiece, his hand scorching a path along her hip on the way to her thigh.

"How I longed to strip you bare and ravish you right here in your aunt's hallway until you screamed out my name?"

She whimpered as his words were having the most devastating effect, never mind his wandering hands.

"James!" She hissed as his fingers found home and slid easily inside.

She moaned and felt his smile against her breast as he tongued her nipple through her nightgown even with the strokes of his fingertips.

He didn't let up until he had her writhing against the clock.

Then she fell apart.

James didn't remove his hand until the last of Miranda's tremors had subsided. He kissed her brow then pulled back with a grin.

"Well, Husband, that was definitely better than my memory serves," she said in a husky voice.

He certainly hoped so seeing he considered it his mission to make up for all the time they'd lost because of his sheer hardheadedness. And looking at his wife's sated expression, he'd achieved that and then some.

"You, dearest, are truly incorrigible," he said.

She cocked an eyebrow. "What can I say to that except I've learned from the very best. And speaking of the best, how about we repair to our room so I can give you *your* early Christmas present?"

He wasn't about to argue, though nothing could top the gift standing right in front of him.

"To that, my love, I would say lead on."

Her responding chuckle was deliciously throaty. "I thought you might say that. Come on then." She took his hand and led him to the staircase. "There's no time like the present."

Tracking the sway of her hips on the ascent, he smiled.

He was exactly where he needed to be—that being wherever Miranda was. He would follow her anywhere.

And with that, life was indeed perfect.

Author's Note

Writing a book is a mammoth task. As such, I'd like to thank my amazing support team.

Firstly, to my gracious editor, Rania Battany. Your invaluable advice helped shape Miranda and James' story into the best it could be. I'm already a better writer for knowing you.

To my family and friends for your unwavering support and encouragement, especially those of you who volunteered to read my (dreadfully unpolished) first draft. I hope you found the finished product very much improved.

To dear Paul, for not even blinking when I suddenly jumped off the couch one evening and declared I was going to write a book. And for never once thinking I couldn't do it. This one's for you.

And last but certainly not least, to you, my wonderful readers. Thank you for taking a chance on this new author. I hope you loved Miranda and James' story as much as I enjoyed writing it.

Happy reading always,
Melissa.

If you enjoyed In Want of An Earl,
don't miss Emily and Marcus' story,
coming December 2026.

About the author

Melissa Finch fell in love with romance after stumbling across her first Mills & Boon in her early teens. Since then, she's found the only thing that trumps reading romance is being able to pen her very own Happily Ever Afters.

Melissa writes the stories she loves to read. Ones of dashing heroines and hapless heroes in desperate want of saving.

When she's not tapping away at her keyboard, you'll find her sipping soy lattes at her local café or combing the library shelves for her next favorite find.

Melissa resides in sunny North Queensland, Australia, with her very own Prince Charming and two Knights-in-Training.

You can read more about Melissa and her writing journey or sign up to her newsletter at MelissaFinch.net.